The Astral Zoo

By Bill Morris

Email: newsunpub@aol.com

New Sun Publications, 227 Granelli Ave, Half Moon Bay, Ca 94019.

Acknowledgments

For my family and loved ones, and, of course, the rest of the zoo.

My thanks.

Bill

"Oh my home, the temple Arkteepa!"

B.

Disclaimer

All of the animals described in this book are fictional. Any resemblance or similarity to human beings you may know is purely coincidental. Besides, they don't look anything like you and I.

B.

✺✺✺ The Jungle

Chapter 1

I am a rockthrower. My tribe lives in the flowering vine-covered temple of Arkteepa. The temple shines golden in the morning as my tribe wakes and begins to forage for our food, as the young scamper from rock to rock, turning over stones for the surprise of insects, or swing through the vines flying like bats. My people live around the temple steps, sit in the sun on its great stones, watching the orange and yellow butterflies, as big as your hand, sail slow as floating dreams around us, as we eat the fallen fruit we find and joke about the dark and terrible thing that lives inside the temple, never seen, only feared. So according to my father, the Watcher, who sits high in the trees ever vigilant for our enemies. It is from this temple that my Grandfather, Chok, father of my mother, Chesed, was hauled away and eaten by the white tiger Gabur.

My name is Tip. Which means the one who calls from the highest tree. And I lived in the jungle temple of Arkteepa. And in the evening sunlight, while the Indian sun sits like a giant red egg in the crowns of the palms, the temple shines ruby red as the calls and stirrings of the night animals rise around us. Arkteepa is my ancient home. But I don't live there anymore.

Now I live in a zoo.

Chapter 2

My grandfather was a Keeper. When I was born he was already no longer a rockthrower, but a simple and respected tender of nests, gatherer of food for the mothers, and keeper of the leapers and hoppers. Even as a hopper myself, I remember him as an elder primate, nearly bald, grey in the chin as the older more pleasant monkeys become. I can't even picture him in the central role of our tribe: a screeching rockthrower, tail up in anger, hustling to find and throw rocks. I only knew him in his Keeper days, a slow, warmhearted animal that had an infectious tilted look of encouragement for the young ones.

I remember Chok sitting on the stream bank, warm in the sun that poured down around Arkteepa, as we wily and skittering young leapt and played in the shallow waters around him in safety. As Keeper he would walk us down to the creek to play in the warm sand banks, show us how to throw sticks into the calm water, showed me the exciting lightening flashes that zigged away from under submerged logs and rocks: fish! We hoppers and leapers would go mad with lust to catch one. The watery flash beneath the surface would send all the hoppers leaping from rock to rock, chasing a flash of excitement, to catch what our young berry-picking and insect-peeling hands could not. We hadn't a clue how to catch one. We hadn't a clue why we wanted to catch a fish. We didn't know the taste and probably wouldn't have liked it. But that zip of energy under the water, it had to be pursued!

And Chok, ever-calm and encouraging, would raise his head and grunt his chuckle of encouragement, meaning, sure you can catch him. You can catch that fish. You nearly got him that time, hopper.

It makes me weep now to think of it. I hear my grandfather saying this to me. Me chocked full of hopper excitement to catch a fish, an eerie little bolt of shining energy below the water. Me, playing happily in the shallow waters with the Keeper near.

Me now here in this zoo.

Oh, Chok, I'm afraid that once I start I'll never stop crying for you.

And here, I weep.

Chapter 3

I remember Chok's death. It's painful for me to think of it. I was so ignorant of death and what I, now a young rockthrower, must do about it. I didn't know, and my family didn't know, and so I learned the slow hard way.

I had grown to be a leaper, tussling with friends on the sandy creek banks, wandering the forest trails, tail up and alert, and on lonely summer afternoons, climbing to the temple's top stones to watch the green and blue jungle valley below. I could hear the calls of the many jungle animals all around. I didn't have my own call yet, though looking out from the temple steps, I longed to call, call to the teeming forest. I knew the jungle, the exotic headdresses of ferns, the vines twisting with a snake's strength when we young'uns swung upon them, the nettles and prickly plants that stung unmercifully, the rotting stumps from which eventually grew the sweetest berry bushes. My brothers and I roamed, foraging the woods for our food and for our interests.

My mother had had other hoppers and so I was free to do all on my own.

Slowly I became an awkward young leaper, soon-to-be rockthrower. My Father, the Watcher, was always in the distant trees, watching. But watching for the safety of the tribe, not truly watching me. So he was not a strong role model as a rockthrower. I had to watch the other fathers to see how rocks were thrown. I had monkey friends, and one randy monkey friend in particular, Steep, who was husky-shouldered and a bit slow of paw. He soon became a champion rockthrower at a young age, under the encouragement of his father, and I watched and learned what I could. Chok was not always around. His foraging and work for the tribe was at some distance from the leapers' runs.

I don't know when I really learned about death. It was certainly as a very young monkey. My mother had told me a story of how, before I was born, her brother, barely a rockthrower, had been hurt in an accident, fallen from the highway of vines that I now traversed with ease, hurt his leg, and was pounced upon by a big white blur. Gabur, the white tiger, had fallen on him and disappeared so quickly back into the jungle lushness there was hardly a remembrance of it.

I had even asked my grandmother once about this death. My grandmother had told me the same story, but with a distance from the incident that there seemed no pain. No pain in the retelling even of the death of a child. As I sat on a rock in the river with my grandmother, whose name I can just remember now, sat with her as if in a boat, the tale of this death was just a story. It had no impact on me. Just something to think about.

Later, I heard more about death. I was now a stumbling young leaper, running with the other monks, playing in jungle schooling. I remember a young female, pretty of face, with nimble long fingers, good at peeling flowers, who wanted to be a Keeper, and played Keeper while I and the rest practiced our monkey antics, pelting each other with sticks and flicking berries. One day, as we played in the classroom of the bushes, some distance from the creek, a hopper, barely able to struggle from his mother's arms, toddled to the creek bed and was squashed beneath an elephant foot. Our little band of leapers heard of this death as just another story, though we tried to guess at the gravity with which we should act.

But this young female, the perspective Keeper, her reaction was the strongest to this unexpected tragedy. She cried. She fancied that had she been closer and a good Keeper, she might have prevented the squashing of this hopper. I and the other leapers could only look on at her perplexed. She believed this story. She was a part of it, and we were not.

Looking back on this now, knowing what I know about death, I look upon this young practice-Keeper and think how preposterous, overly-responsible, and caring!

When death is just a story, then there's no real pain. And I was taken aback by someone who felt pain about this story!

Hoppers, of course, are squashed or lost each year. That's why we have Watchers and Keepers. It's their role to try to prevent it.

But the reality of death, it remained for me something distant, unreal, and yet in the fearful range of possibility, like the roar of Gabur through the jungle trees at dusk. When you heard that sound, and understood it, you never forgot.

Chapter 4

It was often Summers when I spent the most time with Chok. Indeed in late Summers, when the berry picking season had ended, and the torpid stillness of the rainy season approached, I remember going with him to collect sticks to rebuild the tribe's nests before the rains. I had grown old enough to help him drag branches and do as he instructed as I followed him through the forest stillness, dust motes floating in banners of sunlight draped from the high tree limbs. We trod the trails fetching sticks. I was happy to work with Chok, who focused on finding branches and snapping or gnawing them into useful lengths. We tugged and pulled. We bent and snapped. The work of rebuilding nests was done in a comfortable, familiar quiet. When a nest was rebuilt, we sat back on the ground admiring the compact straight lines of the sticks we had assembled. Monkey nests, like hairy armpits high in the tree trunks, things of beauty!

Even at that time I wanted to be a rockthrower. I would practice off on my own, in the privacy of the bushes, believing I was good at it. I had to hide my ambitions from the real rockthrowers, for a leaper throwing rocks, well that could be a cause for laughter, especially a leaper who could not hit his targets, did not even know what the real targets were.

And, of course, the targets are ignorant baboons. The competing species most like ourselves. Animals who packed up and ran in rampage through our tribal home, leaping steps and squawking, stealing our food, killing our young with the practiced wrath of their armies. Baboons, ugh!

And what did I find when I first got to this zoo? Baboons! Everywhere!

But at that adolescent age, I knew nothing about the quest of the rockthrower. I merely had an urge to throw rocks. I threw them at clusters of seedcopters hanging bunched in trees, I threw them at caterpillars inching like fingers pointing, I threw them plunk into ponds, making the bullfrogs bellyflop with fright into the water, into the depths. I was precocious and diligent, but young and really afraid to throw.

I remember one particular afternoon rebuilding nests with Chok when I became angry. He had always encouraged me, been ever-cheerful, saying things like, well, we did that one good, Leaper, whenever I finished a task, no matter how lowly. I was just following instructions. Put this stick here. Moving that rock there. But one afternoon, something happened. I can't remember exactly what. Maybe a stick I had been bending had broken unexpectedly, causing me to fall. Perhaps I had dropped the stick I had struggled to haul up the tree. Whatever the unexpected incident was, I was one pissed and frustrated monkey.

I jumped down and began throwing rocks at the tree trunks around me. Whack, whack! I threw the rocks with quiet fury. Bouncing them off trees and posturing like a baboon, I was mad at something that had happened. And now I'm not even sure what.

I was afraid that Chok would think I was angry with him. But he stood back, slightly surprised by my feisty display, and watched me bang a few angry rocks against trees. Rocks popping like grasshoppers harmless off the bark. And he said nothing.

Somehow, I sensed he just stood back and respected my anger.

It was all right for me to be mad.

He respected my anger. And I realized years later that this gave me the confidence, the hope, that maybe someday I could actually be a real rockthrower.

Something I was afraid to be.

Chapter 5

I sensed that I had ability, the possibility to throw a rock and hit whatever I wanted with a satisfying clunk. But as a leaper, something seemed missing, I couldn't pull myself together, and my aim was off. At the river bank, wishing for the distant, unattained approval of my tribe, I wanted to be a rockthrower with the best of them. I dreamed of heroically throwing a long high rock, beaning a distant baboon, and hearing a satisfying howl rise. My tribe sits up on their haunches, tails curved with pleasure like shepherd's canes, and applauds. I blush and puff up in fulfillment. So, at least went my leaper's dream.

But in truth I barely hit anything.

I picked up boulders too heavy and they fell dismally short. Plop they fell into the river like dropped buckets. I pick up pebbles and they flew off ineffectually like mindless bees. I threw flat stones that took curving boomerang turns toward unexpected targets. Once I hit an elder rockthrower, who howled and turned round, waving a stick over his head, then seeing an inexperienced leaper, angrily kicked my misdirected rock away from him. I felt like hiding in the bushes all day.

A rockthrower's throw has to have a certain elegance to hit its target. A rock of a certain size, no bigger than a monkey fist, must fly in a careful arch to smack precisely between the eyes of an unsuspecting baboon, who for whatever reason had the misfortune to arrive at that instant at that spot. I pursued rockthrowing with a dogged approach, and in return had dogged results.

My throws were in earnest, but lacked art. I could create the beautiful arch, but the target was always left or right of where my rock hit. Dirt flew, my arm hurt, I was unhappy.

But I had a rockthrower dream, and I was trying.

I hid nearly every bit of my efforts from my tribe. I didn't show off for my mother, for my Father, the Watcher, or for the other leapers. What I did would be scoffed at by the newest rockthrowers, the husky-shouldered who wandered about in two and three's, tossing at unwary small animals drinking at the creek, who would bleat in pain and run. These young rockthrowers always seemed to throw best when young females were near.

And if I couldn't throw a rock, then rutting with a beautiful female seemed even more distant. Out of the question!

It is now of some consolation that many other young leapers were like me. Struggling with things they didn't understand and didn't know how to do. I was just so focused on myself, I couldn't see others like me and recognize them. I felt alone.

Ah, but the jungle around Arkeetpa, it has a way of refilling the squelched heart. Each morning, I would rise, and as the blue mists pulled back from jungle and the temple stones lit up with the golden dawn, I looked out and saw the waking forest, the graceful stretched necks of the palms, the low flowering trees with orange and blue blossoms hanging down like colorful birds from the branches. I looked out on the crowded life of the vines, ferns, and elephant-eared leaves blanching with the returning sun, and the creek now glittering. I could hear the distant guinea hens making their rusty crowing as they searched unseen in the bush for food, dewy and sagging spider webs hanging useless and beautiful on the greenery. And here a palm moved, and the head and ear of an elephant came and went out of sight. I knew the eaters were getting up in their dens, the hyenas snarling at their pups. The acrobatic ferrets were already tumbling on their log. The storks militarily strutting to their froggy pools. And there on the berry bushes around the temple floor, the golden butterflies opening and closing, unfolding as if in slow applause for the morning. I could look out from the temple steps, see the verdant and rejuvenating flora and fauna growing wild and free, and feel one undeniable thing: I must call or die.

And I had to go out and throw rocks again.

One afternoon, I was alone throwing and sweating down by the creek. Chok came around from behind a stump and saw me. He sat watching a moment. Despite his presence I kept throwing. And I kept missing. I ran a few steps and tossed only to see my rock fling high over the untouched cluster of orange flowers hung like a beehive in the low branches. My rock cracked down through the branches in the background like a clumsy foot.

Chok reseated himself comfortably on the stump.

I threw again, this time, hurriedly, with all my might. The rock, overly large, slipped from my hand and cracked like a bone against the other creek bed rocks only steps away from me. I squawked. My irritation and frustrations were pumping in my chest. I growled and gritted my teeth. I wanted to quit throwing rocks. And here my Grandfather had seen my vast ineptitude.

I turned to see if he had left yet, disappointed in me, but I was surprised to find him bent over beside me, knuckling through the pebbles and rocks beside me.

Soon he found what he wanted. He handed me a rock, red and hard. It was nearly round, smooth as an egg.

He handed me the rock and said, “Now throw this one, leaper. But you must know something.”

“What?” I said harshly. I was ashamed of myself, and trying to hide it with anger.

“Well, sometimes, it helps to sing a song as you throw. There is a song, the Great Lilly Song, I sang it when I was a young rockthrower. Do you know it?”

I nodded. My mother has sung this song to me. It was a tremendously sad song.

“You can sing it when you must throw.”

“I don’t want to sing a sad song.”

Chok looked at me, pondering my rebuke. Then he shook his head, as if remembering what it was like to be a leaper.

“Of course you don’t,” he said.

“Then I’ll tell you another secret to throwing rocks,” continued Chok after a small pause.

“For now, try this. It is a matter of seeing. Clear your heart and see the thing you want to hit. See the thing within your heart. Then, throw.”

“Why?” I asked.

“Whatever you see in your heart when you throw you’ll hit.”

I had no reply.

“Turn and face your target.”

I did as I was told.

“Now see in your heart the thing you want to hit.”

I looked at the orange flowers hung in the lower branches before me. I looked at them until I could see them in my heart, until I could see my rock hitting these flowers.

“Now throw,” commanded Chok.

I threw.

The orange flowers leapt and flew from the vines like frightened butterflies.

Chapter 6

And that day, as a rockthrower, I learned that you can't just throw, you must first be prepared to throw from within. You must see beyond the throw to the target you want to reach. And you must reach it first from within.

Chapter 7

It was in Summer that Gabur was lurking around the temple. We had heard of him catching and killing other animals in the Viet valley, only several calls away. All the tribe around the Temple of Arkteepa was upset. The killing white tiger had returned. Victims of our tribe were lost. We found only a few bloody bones clumped off the trails or scattered over fallen tree trunks.

There was an air of battle in the jungle.

Our rockthrowers had grown more militant, throwing rocks and making noise in preparation for attacks. The mothers were more watchful, hoppers clinging tightly. It was an uneasy time around the Arkteepa grounds. I was happy that the temple was tall, and solid, and well-laden with rocks. My father was somber and watchful, without a thing to say about the impending threat.

He guessed that I might want to be a rockthrower, though still too young to knowingly face a threat, and circumspectly he remained quiet. He would wait to see if that danger rose before his progeny.

My grandfather, Chok, remained the warm-hearted Keeper. It was as if nothing had changed, this tiger come back into the vicinity of the temple, it was all usual. Life must carry on, the work be done in good spirits, the young watched, the nests tended. The distant threat left distant. Work undone done.

It was that Summer that Chok had eaten some bad fruit that had weakened his stomach. He had been ill and sat in his nest recuperating. Once each day he would walk unsteadily down to the creek banks to take a long drink. There, we leapers and young rockthrowers would see him and gallop over to be near. The other Keepers would sit down, relaxed when Chok had come on the scene.

"How are you, Chok?" I asked sitting down on my haunches before him.

Chok put both his hands on his round distended belly, filled with water from the Temple creek. I could see he was weary, but he was also happy to be recovering.

He sat back on the top of the stump above me and said, "Better. I don't know what I ate, but I ate it. And it nearly did me in, leaper. But I'm better now though."

At this time, Chok was old. My father had told me in secret that Chok would probably die soon. But I was not to speak of it. No one spoke of it, the family just secretly worried. No one thought to talk to Chok about it. The possibilities of Chok's death must be kept from Chok.

I felt uncomfortable with this. This knowledge separated me from him, as a grown rockthrower is separated by knowledge from a hopper. Somehow, my knowing of this death possibility without being able to speak of it to Chok reversed our roles. I was the one who knew something that Chok did not. I had an uncomfortable view of Chok's future, one which Chok was not looking at. He was recovering, it didn't occur to him he would die now.

But I swallowed this bitter fruit and didn't speak of Chok's health to Chok. Somehow the bitterness of that would stay within my stomach for years.

I didn't notice when the birds stopped calling. It was just very still about the creek and sandy pools where the hoppers waded.

I decided to look around for something easy for Chok to eat. I hopped over to where some bland grass, green and tender sprouts, was pushing up at the water's edge. I sat plucking the grass until I had a handful. Now the entire area around the creek bed had gone eerily quiet.

I began walking three-legged back toward Chok, holding my little bundle of healing grass to my chest. A small offering for Chok, but something, anyway. I noticed a nearby Keeper's chin suddenly rise. The Keeper's head turned sniffing. The crowd of running hoppers slowed to a standstill.

I quickly hopped over and stopped in front of Chok with my offering. I looked up at him sitting on the stump above me, about to leap up there myself and give him the grass.

Then I froze. A white head was looking down from behind Chok, who was looking at me, relaxed, unaware of anything behind him.

I opened my mouth speechless. The white tiger was opening his mouth behind Chok. Already I could see white teeth over Chok's head.

Behind me a Keeper screamed. All the hoppers and leapers crouched in that instant of panic and fear before a great flight.

Still unknowing that Gabur was descending on him, Chok looked out bewildered on us.

I was frozen at the sight of the tiger behind Chok. I sat mouth-wide, motionless. I did nothing. I didn't even think of throwing a rock!

And then old Chok began to turn, sensing our fear at something behind him. But too late! Gabur's teeth closed on his head, and picked up Chok like a swaying rag doll. And the great cat turned with its prize and leapt back into the jungle.

In an instant Chok was gone.

And then in the distance I could hear Chok's screams, or perhaps I only imagined his screams, his pain, as he realized Gabur had him. An old monkey realizing alone that he was now certainly food for the tiger.

I was sick and trembling.

This image of Chok's death stayed with me a long time.

Chok carried away by surprise to a dismal death. His cries receding, unanswered in the jungle forest. The other Keepers helplessly, uselessly shooing the hoppers and leapers away from the waters, muddied in our panicked flight.

Back to the Temple.

Back to the Temple where we rockthrowers can secretly weep.

Weep for the loved-ones we didn't help.

Chapter 8

Why didn't I throw a rock?

Why didn't I screech in outrage at a death approaching Chok that no one spoke of?

Where was I?

I was in the paralyzing grip of profound ignorance.

An ignorance I only learned the profundity of later as I watched the deep suffering of the many and talked to the few wise animals here in the zoo.

I didn't even know how to say good-bye to Chok.
I didn't place the white lily on his resting place.
I never even knew whether his bones were found later or not.
I was so ignorant of myself I didn't even know I had to say good-bye.
I just carried on by myself with one less Keeper in the world.
A Keeper I pretended I didn't need anymore.

Monkey ignorance. From rockthrower to leaper to hopper, it's passed on. It so contagious.

Everybody gets their dose. A dose of ignorance of what the monkey animal needs, wants, craves, loves. I pretended. I tried to cover my needs with arrogance, self-centeredness, aloofness, monkey-smarts, uncaring, a whole inventory of things that in the end—

hurt me. Hurt me even more than Chok's unexpected death.

To not even know how to say good-bye to loved ones, well, here in the zoo, that leads to misery and despair.

Chapter 9

So, Chok, here in the zoo, so far from you, so far away from Arkteepa, the golden walls I may never ever see again, here I sing the Great Lily song. The song that my mother sang to me, and her mother to her, and the song that was sung to every heart carried by mother-monkey arms down through monkey history.

The foolish monkey,
his lives in a tree, he lives in a tree,
and he sees his tribe
they suffer, they suffer.
The foolish monkey
he jumps from the tree, he falls from the tree

to go on a great journey
to find the Great Lily.

And with all the power of the great Elephant-God, Keth,
and with all the abundance of our jungle Mother, Binah,
so few of their children,
who journey long
has ever found the Great Lily!

So Rockthrowers, your way is hard,
who throw brave rocks without the Great Lily.
Oh Watchers, your way is cold,
who sit out the night without the heart's glow
of the Great Lily.
Oh Keepers, your way is heavy
who work the Keeper's work without the repose
of the Great Lily.

And the foolish monkey,
he traveled the night beneath the moon,
he traveled the day beneath the sun,
he searched the windy mountain
he searched the sea,
but he didn't find the Great Lily.

Sad was the foolish monkey,
who never found the thing he searched,
Sad was the foolish monkey,
who returned to his home,
Arkteepa! Arkteepa! Though your walls are
falling down, called the foolish monkey,
I, your foolish monkey, have come home.

I have failed my tribe, Arkteepa,

I have failed myself.
I, too, have not found the Great Lily.

And the foolish monkey entered
the temple in despair.
He entered the darkness to hide there.
The foolish monkey entered his temple home
and found the Great Lily, glowing alone!

He has found the Great Lily!
He found the Great Lily! Listen, oh my tribe!
He carries the Great Lily to the trees
where he looks out to call!

And as he looks out on Arkteepa's tower,
the foolish monkey, he holds the beauty
of this ever blooming flower;
And is his heart filled with triumph
because he alone has found the flower?

No, his heart is filled with sadness,
sadness for all those, all those who searched
so long and never found

The Great Lily!

Oh foolish monkey, Arkteepa is your home!
Oh foolish monkey, yours alone,

you hold the Great Lily!

Here, this song has many meanings to my tribe. It sings our pain and our hope. And here, Chok, it means good-bye.

Chapter 10

It was not long after this that Gabur disappeared. We did not know where he went, for a tiger usually stays in his territory for years, moving only miles this way or that, but always present. But Gabur was gone, we no longer heard his hoarse roars in the dusk like a chill wind come quickly through the trees. We no longer saw glimpses of white moving frighteningly swift through the leafy jungle facade. The monkeys as far as five calls away told us that Gabur was nowhere around us.

My tribe relaxed.

But in turn, we began to notice other animals missing as well. A hyena and her litter were gone, cobwebs forming a dirty gate over the opening of her den. Joi, the water buffalo was no longer in the deeper parts of the river. Several storks, parrots, and even a mongoose family were nowhere to be found. Other small animals were disappearing.

There was rumor that man was camping on the edge of the forest.

And though Gabur was gone, men with their cutters and bangers were even more dangerous. They might catch you and kill you for no apparent reason, and even laugh as you died. Unlike rockthrowers, who respond bravely to a threat, their human anger seemed to erupt for any reason and shower down on the unsuspecting animals around them. They seems ready to catch, cut, or kill for reasons we could not comprehend. My Father, the Watcher, once told me it was because they were animals so bizarrely unhappy with themselves. They must all be from neglected and ignorant litters. And if they saw you, they might point a banger and the tree beside you unexpectedly explode. And everyone in the jungle knows, except the worst baboons, that rockthrowers are terrible to eat. We taste like musty hyena pelts! Why would a human attack us?

But jungle lore told us true. The truth and need to stay away from these unhappy animals were certain. Whenever we saw them lugging their boxes along the jungle trails, we did one thing: flee.

My tribe shrank back from the far edges of the forest. We did not want to see what was out there waiting for us. Each day, my Father the Watcher climbed a bit higher in his tree, until he was seated like a furry egg crouched in the top branches.

Chapter 11

My jungle schooling continued as I learned the everyday tasks of my tribe's routine. A Keeper threw a rock, the surrounding leapers threw rocks in imitation. A Keeper stripped a root and ate, we leapers stripped branches and chewed the slippery exposed bones. It was largely monkey see, monkey do. Studious leapers doing without knowing why. If a Keeper had leapt upon a fly and stuffed it up his nose, we leapers would have lame-headed followed along and nostrilled a few flies.

In all I did, I was unremarkable. I might have been a bright student of monkey lore, monkey ways, but without someone like Chok to express an interest in me, without inspiration or the possibility of real reward before me, I was bored, uncommitted, and held back from others. Without someone interested in me, my desires, my secret talents remained uncultivated, unseen. I was a young rockthrower of unremarkable skill. The other Keepers took little interest in me, teaching mostly those they thought were future leaders, superior monkeys trained for their athletic skill and those who are incorrigible numskulls whose antics raised havoc with the tribe and which had to be quelled. Monkeys who shat on the temple stones, producing the grim results of their untaught, unconscious being.

The Keepers didn't know me. To the extent that one Keeper even told me once that I should not be a Rockthrower, I didn't have what it took. I should think of being a Keeper, at best a Watcher. Imagine! Telling a young undeveloped monkey at that age that he would be practically nothing to his tribe. Some Keeper. Why didn't he just hit me in the head with a rock?

Fortunately, because my Father, the Watcher, had unspokenly communicated that I was expected to be a rockthrower, and I didn't believe anything this Keeper had to say, I unknowingly did, I suppose, the most insulting thing to this counselor: I ignored his counseling totally. I look back now on this old Keeper monkey, think of how many other average young monkeys he didn't know and whom he must have counseled toward failure this way, and know the monk was a complete dunce. As our worst rockthrower insult goes, he was a Keeper with a turtle-head. That's a Keeper who pulls his head in first to save himself.

But at the time, I had no anger at this monkey, I had no real feelings of any kind. Without Chok to show the way, I was one very directionless monkey. I couldn't find it in myself to do much, go after what I needed. I was nearly afraid to want anything. If you wanted it, like Chok, it would go away.

At least that's the way I saw it in my black leaperhood.

Chapter 12

However, I had my good days. I remember playing with Steep, the husky young Leaper, a bit clumsy, but well-intentioned, who was bigger and stronger than me. He and I and several over young furred companions enjoyed forming a summer pack and playing about the creek banks. Because of Steep's weight and size, he was naturally the leader of our little group, one that went exploring the leafy jungle trails, the smaller caverns in the Temple stones, the creek wallows. I remember with particular joy how we enjoyed boinking crocodiles with practice rocks as they floats like logs out in the river. When you hit one on the head, the croc would let go a fantastic gysering hiss and flap its tails in a fierce slap on the water as it angrily submerged. Steep, I, and the other would-be rockthrowers would hoot and gibber with glee, dancing our success like sex-crazed storks, flapping our arms and leaping on the mudbanks.

I remember one Summer afternoon our little monkey band had gone to a swing vine that we were using to swoop out over a wider stretch of the Temple creek. Each of our little band would run and leap into space from an overlooking hill, catch the long vine drooping from a high bough, and swing in a long graceful arch out and back over the water. It was a wonderful feeling of launching yourself into nothing, free fall, and then a long glide over the flat creek surface.

Steep was the best, catching the vine in one paw and swinging slowly out over the wide creek. We spent hours running and leaping from the jungle shade and swinging into the hot sun over water.

Then, to our immediate discomfort, a rustling started up in the bushes. Steep, I, and the rest of our little pack, turned, ready to flee a predator. But at the leafy site of the rustling appeared, not a hunter or eater, but three sour-eyed bullish baboons, thick in the haunch and shoulder, wading with superiority into our territory. We rockthrowers sat down with caution. If you did not challenge baboons, and they weren't hungry, then they often tolerated our presence.

It turns out these young baboons had seen us swinging. Envious of our fun, they now wanted to come in and take over the water swing. Ill at ease, conscious that three surly young baboons, larger and stronger than even Steep, were more than our match, we rockthrowers moved aside to sit with caution some little distance away. Having gained the swing without contention, the baboons, of course, were happy with this, that we stayed, because they also wanted to show off.

We didn't like it that by intimidation we had given up the swing, but we had no choice.

The first baboon waded out into the water to pull the vine in, but soon gave up, finding the water too deep before he reached the dangling end of the vine. The other baboons laughed at his wetness. A second baboon, with a scruffy comb of red hair pointing straight up from his forehead, beat his knuckles on the ground laughing and chattering. Then he ran, leapt, and caught the vine as we had, swinging out over the water like a sandbag tied to a rope. But at the end of his ride, he let go too soon. His back and front paws came down on the edge of the creekbed and he stuck with a squish up to his elbows in mud.

Though we were afraid to chatter in laughter, the third baboon, a heavy, aggressive young bull, leapt up and down on his haunches hee-hawing. Before his two wet and muddy companions, he walked with stilted pride, and he prepared to leap out for the swing. Circumspectly, Steep, I and the other rockthrowers said nothing, waiting to see how this threatening young baboon would show off for us.

From his proudly arched back and his long careful strides, I could see he intended to show us what a river swing was for. Baboon style. He intended to swing out farther and higher than anything we puny rockthrowers could ever do.

Slowly he backed up on the high creek bank until he was at the very edge of the jungle. We rockthrowers looked at each other wondering what we would see as this arrogant young baboon prepared to launch himself out on our rock-thrower swing.

In silence, we saw the large baboon charge. Like a running water buffalo, his paws beat across the creek hilltop. In awe, we saw him make a mighty leap into the air. A leap that was as fierce and long as a jaguar's. He sailed high and majestic out toward our waiting vine.

But when he hit the vine and grabbed it, the vine snapped. He fell fifteen feet and crashed into the water, dragging the broken vine down on top of him like a cut rope.

And that instant I knew there was a God!

As the baboon surfaced, screeching his outrage and surprise, paddling in circles, we rockthrowers leapt from our seats cawing with glee. This baboon had dropped like a rock into the water.

We then faded into the jungle before there could be reprisals.

That evening, I called from a high tree that Keth-the-Elephant-God's justice was divine.

Chapter 13

Because it's wet here today, the zookeeper will keep me inside. My cell is a twenty by twenty foot rectangle of glassy white tiles over concrete. Hay is mounted in clumps in mud-colored plastic to simulate the grasslands that we rockthrowers never went near some distance from the Temple. A sorry teepee of sticks is set up in one corner, a lank web of dirty cargo net draped over it, some of the ropes unfrayed like a donkey's tail. And this is a laughable imitation of Arkteepa's jungle vines.

There is a rectangle on the floor filled with dirt, and within the rectangle is a three-foot square pool of old greenish water.

That, I suppose, is their imitation of the Arkteepan creek.

Some days I see it and I want to laugh.

Other days I see and I want to cry.

Chapter 14

The zookeepers have learned from long experience not to put anything like a rock in the rockthrower's cage.

Chapter 15

When I first arrived here, the zookeeper put me in a cage beside another caged colony of rockthrowers. These rockthrowers were long time zoo dwellers. Such that most of their ghostly tribe was born in the zoo, and those who had been captured from their original Indian home remembered little of it.

Their cage was made up of misshapen cavernous walls. The walls had been creamed with gray concrete to simulate their original home in mountains where these wild monkeys had sat on ledges and cliffs looking out over miles of Indian verdure and grassy hilltops. The steep grey walls of their cage were designed to make them feel comfortable, surrounding them with a zookeeper's imagining of this tribe's rocky dwelling. Imagine! Trapping a wild tribe of cliff rockthrowers within a grey circle of concrete, with only a vision of the small monkey-house door before them, when in the wild, what these monkeys lived for, what sustained them, was not the cliffs, but the view of miles of Indian jungle and plains.

Trust a zookeeper to see the cage and not the view!

As a newcomer in my own artificial cage, watching them living in what amounted to a barren, empty quarry, I could only characterize this tribe's behavior as truly depressed.

They mainly sat all day. They had practically no monkey spirit that I could see. Their fur was dull and grey as the concrete surrounding them. They moved in short skitters, watching cautiously around them at all times, for the zookeeper had designed the cage so that at no time was there anywhere for even one monkey to hide. So in their captured state they moved little, using the next strategy of camouflage, trying to be invisible.

And this was my first vision of the other zoo dwellers. I, a lone jungle rockthrower, in a cage just as artificially designed for my tribe. Whew, just thinking about it makes me want to throw up. It was only later, when I learned how caged zoo animals actually live, that I could even tolerate looking around at the other caged and depressed animals during the day.

I didn't realize that actually all of them had the choice of living full lives! At night!

But in my first days in the zoo, this tribe in the grey walls were my only contact with animals that at least seemed to be like me, a bunch of depressed rockthrowers.

I remember watching one rockthrower mother who raised several hoppers in this grey bin. As a picture of motherhood, this was a dismal sight. Although this grey female each year had a new hopper, she had grown up in the cold grey zoo and didn't seem to know how to raise it. She would pick the pale lettuce leaves from the zookeeper's food tins and dangle them before newborn unfocused eyes. She left her new hopper sitting by itself in straw beside her. She would offer the mushy foods that the zookeeper slid in pans through a slot in the wall, not understanding when the hopper turned away. She quickly communicated to them the disease of their cage; useless worry, a life of greyness, lack of hope. If her babies lived to be hoppers, they mainly sat on the floor, clutching their knees and rocking themselves. They seemed on the edge of despair. Their eyes were vacant, and they did not explore. Hoppers without curiosity! That is a hopper's life's blood! I couldn't imagine how that could be. Until I watched how this mother didn't know how to touch or hold her young. They were left alone, beside her, but always distanced, unhugged, unheld, nearly unseen.

And so her progeny didn't prosper.

These hoppers grew up wasted spiritually, growing inexorably into young leapers, and self-sufficient enough to pick up the tasteless foods left on the cage floor, but these monkey's were a sorry sight to one who had seen the fun and wonder of growing up in the Arkteepan jungles. These zoo monkeys knew nothing of the glorious romps at the creekside and vine swinging of my youth. They walked in a furtive, unconfident way. Grey beings produced by the grey surrounding walls of the zoo.

No wonder all of them died.

In Spring, consumption got into the cage, and first the parents, then the young ones died.

I watching them sit motionless, breathing hard, until even the last one, a young monk like myself, dropped over dead on the grey floor.

I turned my back and tried to put this whole tribe out of my mind.

I continued to live solitary in my own cage.

The next one over.

Chapter 16

I sleep and try to avoid the stares most of the day.

Chapter 17

Here is a story of my tribe, the myth of the White Monkey and Kunda. It is a story that is told to all my tribe when they are young, and is to serve as a guidance. It is a story confusing to me. Especially here in the zoo where all we can do is watch each other all day.

It is a story passed by the Keepers to the young. I remember the sunny day beside the creek when a Keeper called all the hoppers about him to tell us of the White Monkey and Kunda, the darkest being that lives in the Temple depths. None of us have seen Kunda, but because of the story, we know Kunda exists, and we fear him, and are ever watchful at evening twilight as we walk the high or low temple stones. You must be aware that if you stray, unwary, on the Temple, what happened to the White Monkey may happen to you. So watchfulness and uneasy treading are a way of life in my tribe.

The White Monkey was named so because he was born with fur indeed white as snow. So white he was a wonder to look at. The elders, Keepers, Watchers, rockthrowers, and curious young came just to look at him when he was only hours old. He slept quietly in his mother's arms, and was docile and mild when the adults inspected him to be sure that he was indeed part of the tribe.

He grew up as just another monkey among us, but always an object of some teasing. The younger hoppers and leapers can be cruel to anyone who is different from our tribe's norm. And this monkey was visibly so different. He was white as snow in a world covered with green vines, grasses, brambles, and jungle flowers.

So he grew up being slightly apart from the other members of tribe. Because of the teasing, he became something of a philosopher. Really, a philosopher monkey, that is rather funny isn't it? I mean monkeys are meant for the set roles of our tribe, Keeper, Watcher, Mother, Rockthrower. And yet here was a white monkey, surviving somewhat on his own, who was none of these. He was just a good kind monkey.

And he eventually began to teach the other young monkeys around him. He taught wise things: that teasing creates anger, creates the want for revenge. That rock throwing at your brother creates rockthrowing come back at you. In all, that being a good monkey is a better way than being bad.

Simple lessons, really, that the tribe heard and liked and tried to follow.

The White monkey's reputation for wisdom grew.

My tribe had never had a monk who could communicate so clearly what the tribal heart wanted to hear. It was a rough jungle out there. Tigers, hyenas, and other eaters could catch and kill you in a second. We had hard rainy seasons where it was impossible to find food. We had cold and sickness in other seasons. Rockthrowers often fought among themselves. So hearing the White monkey's stories helped the tribe, it eased the burden of jungle life.

Many wished they, too, were white monkeys. To be white and wise like him! To not wear this dull brown coat!

And then he gave his greatest lesson. The White Monkey called to all the tribe, and they gathered at the foot of the temple and looked up to the high stones where the white monkey told them something to gladden their hearts. He said he saw his tribe suffering in fear of Kunda, the unseen black being that dwelled within the temple. Kunda the silent, crawling one, who could secretly snatch hoppers, leapers, and even adults from temple stones, and they were gone. Another member of our tribe mysteriously disappeared, without bone, fur, or blood left to signal the missing animal's existence.

Our tribe members wished to not have Kunda always part of the tribal life. Living in the jungle was at times hard enough, but to have to fear a lurking black being within the very temple, too. That was just a heavy burden for the monkey heart to bear.

So the White Monkey called down to the tribe. And he said, "If you raise a pole at the top of the Temple, I will sit upon it. And I will protect you from Kunda. I will watch for him and protect you. You, my tribe, can follow my simple lessons and live happily, and not have to fear Kunda any longer."

This was a message to gladden any monkey heart.

It is said that my people rejoiced, the young ran and swung from the vines squealing with excitement all around. The elders nodded, this was indeed a good idea. A watcher to watch over the tribe solely to save us from the unseen Kunda. They would not have to worry about Kunda any more.

And in a day, a long pole was found, dragged by many monkey arms to the top of the temple and set up straight, high over the temple.

And indeed that day, the White Monkey climbed the pole and sat upon its very top.

And the tribe members, mothers and rockthrowers alike, felt good that they now didn't need to worry about being on the temple stones any more, they had someone always watching to save them from Kunda.

And so the whole tribe slept well that night. The White Monkey was sitting high on his pole, protecting them. Protecting them from the black, crawling being that they feared lived within the temple.

And the next morning the tribe woke up, refreshed, happy, and looked around themselves in peace. And then they looked up at the pole where the White Monkey looked down on them.

And the pole was empty.

The White Monkey was never seen again.

Word passed through the tribe that Kunda had eaten him.

So every young monkey in my tribe learned that no monkey can look out for another. You have to watch out and take care of Kunda yourself.

So the story goes.

Chapter 18

I don't exactly know how it happened, how I was captured. One day I was trotting down the jungle trails I had trotted down so many times in my leaperhood. At each instant that I spotted a rock that had good throwing potential, I sat down to pick it up, then looked about for an acceptably interesting target. I had grown to be a better shot. At least I should hope so after throwing thousands of rocks at anything so unfortunate as to move before me. I could now fling rocks and scruff the tail feathers of the lime-green parrots, who squawked, shat, and flew away with angry undignified wing-beats. I threw long distance rocks that stuck like stone eyes in the crumbling totem poles of termite nests. I even tried to kill fish. I remember, in a pack of three leapers, sneaking to the lip of a jaguar's den and tossing in a wet stone and the thrill of hearing a snarl return out of its darkness. How we frazzled leapers ran like hell to hide! From the top of a palm, I had once even beaned a hyena who dropped over unconscious on its side for an hour. What pride I took in that!

And after each successful throw, I would scramble to the top of the highest tree and call out my mighty victory.

Secretly I even beat my chest a bit like a gorilla.

Rooster pride.

Foolish memories, I can see why adult rockthrowers might giggle at me. But that's all right, these things, they sustain me a bit when in the zoo here. When I feel blue.

Every once in a while I made a very beautiful call. Other monkey's told me that they had heard and liked my call. They said my calls were long and melodious, and seem to haunt the jungle.

The jungle I was about to leave.

I had stopped alone to pick up a rock. There, beside the trial, was a piece of fruit. I dropped my rock and hopped over to it. I also sensed something else there, a smell that I didn't recognize. It was only later that I learned that the smell was man. Then something snared my foot and jerked me into the air.

A day and a half later, me falling in and out of consciousness hanging upside down as I labored to even breath, two tobacco-stinking hands took me down.

I doubt my tribe ever knew what happened to me.

Chapter 19

I came to enough to find myself in a burlap sack. After a bumpy hour, the sack top opened and a human hand descended and grabbed me firmly.

I was lifted out of the sack and I saw I was in the man's camp, stacks of boxes and caged animals scattered and disorganized everywhere. There the mother hyena and her litter were pacing in a bamboo cage. In a small box, cloaked with thin meshed wire, were a mongoose family pushing their sensitive noses through the screen. The place reeked of burning wood. Ragged women were squatting and cooking and men were lifting and tugging boxes that held frightened animals, and poking into the cages with sticks.

I screeched and clung to my captor's arm as if it were a briskly swaying tree branch.

I was carried over to a larger cage with bamboo slats tied with twine that held other animals. I could see I was going to be put in this cage. When I looked closely into it, I saw several other forest monkeys, green spider monkeys, unlike me, and even two or three baboons. The idea of being put in this cage with several baboons made me nauseous with fear. I screeched more and tried to struggle up the man's arm to escape.

I was taken to the open door of the cage and handed over to a smiling woman who was going to put me in. The impending fact of being left alone in this cage with other unknown animals grew too much. I screeched and clawed at the woman firmly holding me. The woman who had me, laughed embarrassed as she tried to shake me off, but I was too firmly attached. I clung like a mitten to her wrist and would not fall off into the cage. To assist her, another human put an arm through the cage slats and reached out and caught my arm. I was slowly being pulled into the cage by the paw as the other woman pulled back trying to make me release my hold. I hung in the cage door stretched in a Y between the two pulling humans. I was so afraid, I was crying and clung to the woman. At that point I would have done anything to be with my mother!

The other monkeys and even the squatting baboons were watching this scene with ill ease.

Finally the hand within the cage succeeded in dislodging me from the arm I clung to and pulled me in.

I dropped to the cage floor alone. I hopped over to a corner and sat trying to hide from the eyes of the other strange animals in this cage.

The other animals, even the baboons, moved uneasily away from this shivering newcomer.

Thus, I entered and spent my first day in a cage. One of many on my journey to the zoo.

Chapter 20

I sat for what seemed like years in that cage, looking out through the bamboo slats at the jungle to which I could not return. I suppose it was only about two weeks that I was held in there with the other bewildered primates, slumping now with the boredom. We were given bad food and the forced discipline of our containing box was taking its toll. I had only been in the cage a few days when I felt the spring in my legs drain from me. But it seemed like I was in there for ages. It doesn't take long for a cage to knock the piss and fire out of little monkeys. Even the captured baboons were sitting like slump-shouldered hulks most of the day.

Occasionally a kind-faced woman would give us plates of drooping greenery and left-over samples of their human foods.

Even their bananas were old—yellow and mushy as slugs.

Gahhh!

I learned to sit still. I learned to be quiet. I learned to lift my arm to take down the droopy food from the human at the top of the cage.

What a squashed life for a monkey.

I remember once when a young girl with mousy face and clear round spectacles came and sat beside my cage. She wanted to play with us and teach us tricks. I remember her coaxing voice as she tried to call me over to her. Then I saw her hold out in her hand a white, tender string of root. I hopped over to get it. She held the root just near enough to the cage so that when I stuck my arm out, I could almost reach it. But then she jerked the root-string away. I pulled my arm back in and sat confused. She'd offered a root, but not given it to me. Again she put the root near the cage. I reached out again. I stretched in pain to get it. She pulled the root away and sat looking at me. She wanted me to stick my arm out the cage once more. I put my begging arm out. She dangled the root just over my open palm. Then she took it away. I sat down frustrated to tears. Why hadn't she given it to me? Like a female, she was offering food to eat, but keeping it back. I looked unhappily around at the other monkeys, but they were no help. I needed this food, and I couldn't get it.

Then the spectacled girl reached out and put the white root close enough that I finally approached her and she let me grasp it in my palm. With my prize I hopped to the other side of the cage. I sat down to inspect and eat it.

It was a piece of string.

Chapter 21

The next day, the humans broke camp and we were all carted away many miles. The last sights and smells of the Arkteepan jungle left the cage.

Chapter 22

I was grabbed by the scruff of the neck and transferred into another small bamboo cage. This one was just big enough for one monkey, not much larger than a bushel basket. I couldn't leap; I just had room for a small hop. All I could really do for exercise was grasp the bamboo bars and sway left and right. This little cage was hauled to the top of an old hawking and grunting truck, which set off on a bumpy night journey, me swaying worried on top of the heap of other captured animals and their cages.

The next day at dawn, we arrived at a port city. The truck pulled directly into a warehouse with great high rafters. Like a flabby jungle, burlap netting was hung over every window, hole, pipe, or crack that a monkey or bird might make an escape for. The interior was a large spacious cavern of cages, boxes, and dirty equipment. There was a heavy smell of old dry animal feces, oil, and something else...sea water. These were all uneasy new scents for my sensitive jungle nose.

A large open door stood on the other side of the warehouse where I could see a steel wall, which I learned later was the hull of a ship. Through this door came a continual line of workers carting boxes on their heads, lugging tools, or hefting cages pulled and pushed away between several workers.

The warehouse, dark and old, was eerily quiet, with the sound of tapping and hammering, yelled orders, and an occasional human grunt. Hard work was going on here and no one was happy about it. It was also surprisingly quiet considering the great dismal structure was filled with animal cages, each animal lying low and tense.

I didn't know what was going to happen. But I had had enough. I stood up on my hind legs and screeched and screeched. I just screeched, not even a call.

The other animals began stirring, emitting short growls, squawks, and cries, a few making frustrated lurches within their boxes.

A man with stringy black hair picked up a long stick and began whacking the sides of the animal cages to get our attention and make us shut up.

That was our first day in animal purgatory.

Chapter 23

I spent three days in this dim warehouse, watching the sweating humans walk to and fro. At night, when it was time for sleep, weak overhead lights came on, and the humans continued their toil. I couldn't sleep, for with the lights, continual movement, and dark shadows bleeding from the cages onto the dirt floor, the warehouse became a threatening place.

A sullen aura was cast by the silent cages around me.

As cages were pushed out the black door, I became more tense.

Then I saw something slowly weaving out of a black hole in the floor.

It moved silently, like the thick muscle of an arm bending and unbending, as it pushed itself along.

As it passed the foot of each cage, it turned its head and looked in. The cage remained black and silent. Then after several seconds of stillness, the animal pushed off again, continuing its slow hunt.

It was some sort of water python, with no colors, its skin the same brown shade as the dirt.

Carefully, it kept its muscular form within the black shadows of the cages.

And it was crawling my way.

I scuttled back.

My cage was perched on several boxes so I could see down upon the snake. As I continued to watch, the silent animal began sliding up over several boxes and then began turning my way. I knew it was coming up to investigate the smell from my cage!

It was curling on the box before my cage now. It was stopped. I could see it was much larger than I. As its brutish head stared uncaring in at me, its mouth was slightly open, as if scowling or angry at something unseen. I could see a sharp tooth, a fang for stabbing. I froze with fear. I sat completely still in the rear of my cage. I didn't blink, breath, or move. In the small box I was in, absolute stillness was my only chance. Its head began to weave back and forth. I could tell that it was a young snake, yet nearly blind. It was hoping for some movement in the cage to signal that it should attack.

I was alone, in a dark box, without my tribe behind me. I could not call for them. I was boxed in and defenseless in this ugly warehouse jungle. I sat still as still can be. I held so still that my eyes unfocused, the surrounding blackness seeming to seep inside them, as I remained as motionless as I could.

The snake raised its head to look down on me. It posed there motionless for several seconds.

Then its mouth closed, the fang that I saw disappeared, and the animal turned and slid off in another direction.

I swallowed. I remained still in my cage.

Ever since then, I've had great distaste for and suspicion of snakes.

And so I learned the first fundamental lesson of being in this world run by man. In this warehouse jungle, when faced by danger, by unexpected violence, be still, be passive and as invisible as you can. Then danger may pass you by.

Imagine, in the Arkteepan jungle, where fleeing, ferocity, and quick action — where alarming the group to group action—were the rules for saving your life, here in this civilized jungle, where you were confined, could not escape, and were faced by an enemy, the opposite rule applied. Sit still, be passive in hopes that the problem wouldn't notice you.

What a horrible lesson for a monkey to learn: the first law of the zoo!

I sat blinking away my fear. Shivering, I couldn't even call out to the jungle and my tribe to release my pent feelings.

I had to swallow my fear and my anger and my need to throw rocks. I had to sit in that cage and do nothing.

Deep went my monkey pain.

Chapter 24

The next day, as the sun came up, the activity of moving cages out of the warehouse renewed and intensified. Somehow a current of impending departure was in the air, and it conveyed itself as anxiety in my stomach.

More workers seemed to be struggling with larger cages, and straps and chains were being laid around many containers.

A man in a khaki shirt and shorts was standing in the warehouse midst like a music conductor directing the action with a short stick. His cries and directions were answered by hoots and yells from the workers about the periphery of the warehouse.

A crew of three brown workers in ragged shorts and black shirts walked from cage to cage throwing handfuls of floppy or grainy foods between the bars. I saw a dead chicken or two tossed into the larger cages and the feeding crew abruptly jump back.

As if a jungle cat couldn't tell the difference between food and a disgustingly greasy human arm. Stuffed up in a cage myself, I knew that the only reason I'd touch such an arm would not be to eat it, but to yank it off. If I just were a panther.

Perhaps that's what the feeding crew really was aware of.

They weren't the food, they were the potential victims.

As the hours passed that day, and the warehouse slowly emptied, I became aware of a cage holding a pair of marmots next to me. They were a male and a female, and as the hours passed and the loading workers worked their way closer and closer to our cages, I noticed the male marmot getting more and more nervous. The female seemed to be becoming passive, slinking to the cage corner. Every once in a while, the male would rush to the corner and hastily mount her. He would rut with her and then return to his frantic pacing.

As the day went on this rutting happened time and again. It was like a cycle, the mounting pressure of cage anxiety, the lack of protection of the tribe, the exposure, and the blocked ability to flee or defend, set these animals into a cycle of repetitive behavior. It seemed like behavior for distraction, behavior for behavior's sake.

Why were they doing that? Were they really desperate to procreate within that cramped cage? Then I realized, that this was not absurd behavior in the face of their situation, surrounded by intense feelings and a lack of control. These animals had returned to following a first law of the jungle: when in the face of threat, failure of your abilities, separation from your tribe, in the face of hopelessness, no matter what the absurdity in consequences, you must struggle to reproduce, establish a relationship. Create a new tribe.

Build a new world from the beginning.

It's just some of these jungle laws make you look pretty funny in a little city of cages.

Chapter 25

They put me in a box. It was cold and dark in there, with one little window that looked out on the dark and damp interior of the ship's hold. I could hear the rustle and snarls of the other trapped animals all around, frightening, for I could hear a panther's heavy panting just next to my cage—an eater of monkeys, next to me, caged in the dark! I was at first in horror, looking out on the other boxes, each containing its wild animal, all stacked in the dimness, hearing only their cries and seeing desperate eyes haunting the wire webs nailed over their box windows.

I was alone. Alone in the four stiff corners of a box in the interior of a ship, surrounded by other boxed animals. I sat, my cries for my mother unheard, my yells for my father, the Watcher, unnoticed, my desperation for the warmth of Chok, my long dead grandfather, burning inside me. After two days in this box, I became depressed. After three days, I prepared to live in this dark box for years. The cries of the other animals subsided around me in my depression.

And I felt terribly alone. A little monkey is nothing without his tribe. And I was nothing. I felt my desire to be free, to be in my mother's arms, to be in the goodhearted company of my grandfather burn in a small constant flame inside me. A small flame that was in danger of going out. I didn't understand any of this. Although I was a rockthrower, I felt young, barely more than a hopper. Not yet a leaper. And I seemed to have no hope of becoming a rockthrower.

Sitting in the dark, I wrapped my arms around my knees folded up at my chest, and I sat alone, wondering why this was, how should I change to get free, to make this better. I hadn't a clue. Every once in a while a carrot was pushed through the stiff webs of the little window.

It was soft and chewed like flesh. I felt I was eating my own bones.

And slowly the hold rocked, tilted at sea, like the moon carried on the back of the slow walking Keth, Elephant God, source of all monkey power, who carries the sun and moon on his back once across the sky each day. But in this hold, there was no sun or day, no moon. Just the suffering of the other animals, which had quieted now, and which felt around me like a slow pulling strain. Even the panther's high woman's screams of revenge had faded in the dark, replaced by a frustrated bumping of the cat's tail switched against the box sides. I knew if it ever got out it was going to kill something.

Then time disappeared. I had no sense of time or day passing, or nights descent, no sense of when to eat, where to go next. There was none of these. So time disappeared. I had no idea if a day or year had passed as I sat, clutching my knees to my chest, staring into the dimness, dreaming, dreaming of my mother's arms, gone, and hearing my grandfathers cries as he was dragged away by Gabur into the forest, the cries unanswered by me, as he left for his death. Killed by the white tiger. Oh, I could hear them now. I could hear them.

Then I realized what I heard were my own cries. I was screaming at the little window.

Chapter 26

After a week, the smells changed. From anger, panic, and confusion, now I could tell somewhere in the dark an animal or two had given over to despair and died. The smell of the dead hung around us and the flesh-eaters became more restless for they lived by fresh meat and the smell of bad food drove them to retreat even when they could not. The urinary smells from the different boxes were worrying to the quick-footed, the runners, and the leapers, who from it could recognize their enemies, cooped and growling around them. But the background smell of the dead animals kept all harassed and watchful. I held still and slept, straining through sleep to wake from this eternal waking dream, be freed of this black cage, in a tilting ship moving without a trail to follow, somewhere, full of jungle animals without freedom.

It was after the eleventh or twelfth soft carrot, pushed into my cage like a dead finger pointing inward, that I gave up eating all together. I didn't want food any more; it wasn't the right food. I sat in my little box, knowing that the beautiful world of Arkteepa was out there, the climbing stones, the free-swinging vines, the free waters flowing clear with the scurry of frightened fish in the shallows, those great flames of curiosity and youthful wonder still existed in Arkteepa, but not for me. The little organization of my life was now hopeless in a black box. I waited, fasting, for someone, my mother to save me.

Each day no one came.

The thing I needed as a young leaper were missing. I sat waiting to die.

And then a remembrance came to me as I daydreamed alone in the dark. I remembered waking once in my mother's arms, late late in the dark of night, to see a strange light wobbling through the forest below. I raised my head from my furry mother's arms, she sleeping with her back against the tree trunk in our nest, and watched as this light moved through the forest and came slowly up to the temple. When it reached the temple steps, I saw sleepily it was a young boy, seven or eight, who was wandering in the jungle in the dark of night, holding a candle before him, which only lit his way a few feet ahead. When he came to the temple, he sat upon the first stone, and turned out toward the jungle, and with the candle in his lap, he sat.

He simply sat looking into the darkness.

I knew he was lost. Little monkeys can recognize lostness even in humans. I saw that he was tired and lost and he was such a sad little boy. As I watched from the treetop, I could see all he had to protect him was the little lit candle. And it was burning down. And the boy seemed resigned. He sat, sad and alone, watching the jungle blackness around him, waiting for the candle to go out. I knew if the candle blew out he would die. The jungle blackness and the fierce things that lived there would come in and bring his end. And then, being small myself, I went back to sleep in my mother's arms.

I don't know whatever happened to that little boy.

I don't think his mother or father ever really found him.

And when I woke in the blackness of my own little box, remembering the lost boy on the temple steps of Arkteepa, lost, unmoving, unfound, I realized with fear and nausea, it was happening to me. Oh, Grandfather, find me! The Keeper, I need you. But you too are dead. The Watcher is not near. My mother distant and untouching in my home. It was beyond their monkey powers to find me now.

In my heart, I knew the truth of being lost. It is not just not knowing where to go, but worse, it is also having no one looking for you.

Chapter 27

Once each day the dark sky opened. Down shown a blinding blue light as the cargo hatch moved. The cold air descended in a breeze from on high flushing out the dank and terrible odors of the animal hold. I sat blinking, looking out my little box window like a bewildered prisoner caught sleeping.

Then I could hear slow movements in the other boxes. It was similar to the sounds of my tribe waking and stirring in the morning. Except in a few short moments each of the animals, coming to consciousness, turned once around in their box to discover this was not their den, there was no exit, and different growls, snarls, and intense scratchings erupted here and there.

I put my nose to the wire, looked into the beautiful blue sky, and sniffed the fresh air deeply. It was not the rich jungle air that was vitamins to my blood. It was the thin air of the sea. Yet I stared up at this great rectangle of light hung in the dim overhead, wishing I could climb up, climb out of this hold.

And the daily appearance of this blue light, perched overhead in the otherwise continual darkness, became a God to me. Not a sumptuous and surprising god of Arkteepa, where the gods throw down fruit to you as birds chatter from on high, nor one of the raging gods that sent packs of baboons running rampant through our midst, breaking branches, challenging, snarling to kill our young ones for meat, which set our hearts and bodies running to the rock piles to throw rocks with an exquisite anger —ah, I remember throwing rocks at baboons with a hardy feeling that can only be called joy! I was a rockthrower, and by the jungle gods you red haired, sharp-tooth fool baboons would know it! No, it was not one of the wondrous jungle gods who always killed with a pounce that brought defeat and death in less than a minute. Not the gods that poured misty water over a waterfall into a deep green pool, caped with flowers in rainbow colors and vines come down to wade at the water edge, where to merely drink was to refill one's spirit with the wondrous song of the jungle. Those gods of riches, abundance, cruelty and love, sun's warmth on your fur, and eerie howls at night, those gods were far from me now.

No, that blue light above, distant and austere, was a god I could only worship from afar. It shown above to me as with some message, but a message I forever guessed at. Why was I here? Tell me, I would think, give me sign of care, of direction. As I sat in my box, this blue rectangle, with its cross of sunlight in the middle, was distant and watching, moving slowly overhead in a balanced rhythm, shining the same above all the animals, not just me. Why had this God grown distant, why was this God not working for me? To me it was the chance for Arkteepa. But I could never reach it. I was locked in a box. This God shown down once a day, over all the animals the same, as if putting us all under a cruel justice, that gave each animal the same brief sight of the sky, the same unhappy food each day, no matter whether you were large or small, beaked or clawed. This God controlled all and had us all in the same box. I wanted some special message for me. But none came other than from my own imagination. I became a passive animal under this distant blue light, waiting for it to come, to bring change, to open a way. All I could do was wait.

In my young suffering, I didn't know that a passive animal is no animal at all. My father, the Watcher, had once told me in a sad tone that a rockthrower who never learns to throw rocks can live in sadness all his life. Not even knowing what is missing! Even he, who was not a rockthrower, but a Watcher, knew this! For if you are a rockthrower, you must throw or die. It is in your blood. That is the internal law.

But it is a law this blue light, withholding the jungle riches, would never teach.

Why had my rich jungle gods abandoned me and left me this insipid blue square to pray to? And as I looked up at it, my nose to the wire of my cage, I could only pray for mercy with all my monkey heart. And I realized that this blue square God was distant and watching like my father, watching overhead, providing security within this darkness, watched over but with a sense of being unprotected, leaving us in an ignorant darkness of ourselves, what we were and what we could do as wild animals. In this hold, we weren't jungle animals. We were stacked boxes. We had no animal capabilities whatsoever. We were like a collection for this God on high, stopped from chewing flowers, stopped from charging in wrath, stopped from picking fleas, rutting at the first opportunity of a raised rump, stopped from howling with pleasure or agony, stopped from growth. And as I feared, I was on my way to man's civilization. The one thing my father was most watchful for! For he knew man had once built the temple of Arkteepa and then abandoned it. Abandoned it to us. And yet, he also knew that, every so often, they must come back, back to its warms steps, to see the ancient temple in the grip of the jungle vines, feel it around them, stand in awe before it, or pray to it if they can remember how. And my job was to screech from the highest steps and throw rocks. Guarding the treasure that was ours.

Chapter 28

"What are you doing out there?" I asked. I was straining to look through the wire web of my box into the dim ship's hold. There, nosing about between the boxes was a spotted leopard. I was speechless. This animal was outside of its cage.

"I'm looking around," said the leopard, "This is certainly a noxious place. The animals bedraggled and poorly fed. I wouldn't want to munch one even by mistake."

The leopard jumped to the top of a box and stood looking around like a ballerina on a platform.

"Who are you?" I said.

The leopard shrugged. Then, like a stork reaching underwater for a fish, the leopard's head disappeared through the wooden top of the box as it looked inside, then quickly pulled its head back out.

"Croc," said the leopard with some distaste, "I hate those."

The cat sat down and began to lick its paws. I was astounded at what I had seen. How could an animal put its head through wood and look into another's cage like that?

"Who are you?" I asked.

"Just another animal like you," replied the leopard, "but unlike you, I've already lived in a zoo. I'm just being transported to a different one. Heading for the same life in a new cage, so to speak."

"What's a zoo?" I asked.

The cat laughed sarcastically as I watched bewildered.

"How did you do that? How did you get out of your cage?" I asked. Desperation had unexpectedly entered my voice.

"Sleep on dreamer," smiled the leopard, "You have a lot to learn."

And then I woke. I had been dreaming in my box. All around me were the same closed boxes. Every animal was still locked in its cage, buried alive in the metal belly of the moving ship.

And somewhere I heard a leopard's hiss of laughter.

I felt sick at heart, such was my disappointment.

Chapter 29

It was the third week when I sensed the rocking had stopped. With the ocean scent coming down from the hatch cover, I now caught the fragrance of land, burning charcoal, the cooking scents that I had met when exploring too close to the cutters' camps, those ragged bands that cut down the Arkteepan forest. And I heard the frightening yells of civilization starting up out of sight. I sensed the change with a slight anticipation and the fear that being too near humans always gave me.

When the hatch cover groaned back that day, the surrounding animal boxes were eerily quiet. Although from my little window I couldn't see all around, and didn't know what to expect, I heard the clump of dropped ropes, the rattle of chains, and muttering humans clumping and shoving boxes around us. I pressed my nose to the wire window to see the smaller boxes being hauled up out of the hold.

The hatch cover had been thrown wide open and a hot patch of sun had fallen directly on my box. I felt the sun on my face and felt relief. It was a steady intense heat, but I welcomed it after days of damp twilight in a metal hold. I began to hope that I too would be winched up out of this pit, the gut of this terrible ship.

And my turn came. I felt hands tying lines to my box, and up, up and away I went, swaying high, as if sitting in the tops of the palms watching out over Arkteepa. I felt the urge to call to my tribe, but could not. The box was turning like a crazy compass needle and I really didn't know which direction I was facing when it came down to rest on the deck.

Outside in the fresh air, I clung to the little window, looking out with great amazement. In the distance, at the end of a long wharf crowded with crates and netting, I saw a great hillside of white boxes, shops and houses, interspersed with palm trees, and the smell of languid sewage, farm animals, rotting fish, and heat baked wood and cement. I could see humans in white robes, in dirty work clothes, children prodding donkeys in the streets. So many people, I had never seen so many on their feet in streets before.

From the chatter of the other animals on deck, I found out that this was no longer India. This was greatly different land in Africa.

Morocco.

Chapter 30

Bustling around us, poorly clothed in dirty work pants and buttonless shirts open to the waist, men were working among the boxes. Some unshaven, wearing gray cloth turbans, a work crew of men was lugging and shouting at each other. I'd never seen such men before. They were always talking as they worked, never seeming to agree. Except for an occasional eruption of laughter.

Arabs!

And that white city on the hillside was Tangiers.

I looked out on the deck, the wharf, the distant city, wanting to be anywhere but here in this box. Something about the high castle-like structure on the far right, the Kasbah as I learned later, its plastered mud walls going up to the hilltop, higher than the surrounding choir of white and blue boxes, reminded me of the great overlooking tower of Arkteepa. As I looked at it, I saw a distant freedom.

The crew continued to rattle the chains and haul the ropes. The fresh air in my lungs was re-invigorating me. I heard some of the fiercer clawed animals give short experimental roars. Testing the air to see what fear could be instilled.

Cooped within my box so long, I felt little fear of them, only a cramped apprehension. Then I noticed a little girl in a blue dress and white apron walking fearlessly among the crew members and boxes on deck. She was thirteen or fourteen, the Captain's daughter, and she walked about the boxes looking in each one. She was not afraid to approach the boxes, not even the biggest ones. She walked with a stiff authority. It was an authority the Arab work crew obviously deferred to. She spoke to them in clear French, and the older Arab men looked down on her with kind eyes, bending to her will. They bent to move boxes for her, give her access to others, brought the carrots and vegetables she occasionally pushed into the wire windows. The girl smiled and was cordial about the differential treatment she received. It seemed the crew enjoyed honoring her by serving her, because she was different, a child, and serving her was not a requirement, but a gift. Men, who by honoring this daughter, were honoring their own daughters.

The little girl in blue dress and white apron came my way and looked in my little window. I saw her see me, smiling, and exclaim:

"Quelle singe! Si mignon!"

Evidently she was pleased to find me, a small under-developed rockthrower looking at her in return.

She looked in and whispered her strange but welcome words into my box. I didn't understand them, but just to have words coming at me was a great relief, a pleasure like the sunlight of Arkteepa falling on my shoulders.

Evidently, because I was interesting, the Captain's daughter wanted to feed me. She called for an old Arab to lumber over and bring the food. I heard her cajoling the old man, who was shaking his head gravely. I watched in amazement as the girl's forehead furrowed in consternation, badgering the old bristle-chinned man into behaving.

Shaking his head, the old Arab shrugged and bent to the box. I could hear his hands fool with the latch, untwisting the sealing wire.

A hinge creaked.

The top of the box lifted.

I didn't hesitate.

Like a jack-in-the-box, I sprang out of the box with all my might. I heard a squeal of surprise from the girl, and as I hit the metal deck, I saw in the corner of my eyes the girl's shoes jump back. I had an inner energy even she had not suspected. My leap had surprised her and even the old Arab. I scrambled across the metal deck toward the rail, now hearing the warning shouts of other Arabs seeing my escape. I was not afraid, I was moving. In one bound, I shot to the top of the ship's rail.

And like any monkey with close pursuers, and no time to check ahead, I leapt high out into the empty air.

At last chance, when a desperate monkey leaps, he has to believe as he reaches blindly, falling to the unknown, that a tree will appear beneath to save him.

Chapter 31

I fell twisting through the air, waving my arms and cycling my tail. Trying with monkey skill to keep myself upright and balanced.

I fell fifteen feet and splashed into water.

Warm water all around. Salty!

I bobbed to the surface, monkey paddling. With distaste, I began swimming hardily to keep my head above the surface. After one quick circle for orientation, I spotted the wharf pilings with their shade and tree-like trunks, and swam toward them where a shadow spread that reminded me of forest safety. Behind me, above the steel wall of the ship's hull, I could hear yelling coming down from on high.

I reached a piling and scrambled up. I pulled myself up into the wooden under structure and sat in safety on a tarry beam. Hastily I looked around me at the mysteriously straight and narrow causeways under the Arab wharf. I could hear trampling feet echoing across the gang plank and thumping overhead my way.

I shook myself out like a wet dog. A straight highway of beams led away under the peer toward the Arab city. Now I could see Arab heads, like balloons with upside down faces, descend and look around as their owners hung by their bellies over the edge of the wharf and peered into its shade for me.

I had no rocks to throw. And besides, these squinting watchful faces were above me.

I turned and jogged the beams, heading for the Kasbah.

Chapter 32

The Kasbah is an awkward place for a monkey. The streets even alleys teem with people in robes, plodding donkeys, turning spoke-wheeled carts, cats, rats, refuse, women lugging upside down bouquets of fully-feathered chickens by the legs. Taxis honk. Walking street criers call their wares: Sardines! Milk! Junk! Men walk around like ambulatory totems with rugs, clothing, multicolored bead strings, even goat-skin bags of water draped over their selling arms and backs. The smells of charcoal, sewer, cooking smoke, honey, orange blossoms, rotting fruit rinds overwhelm you. Cripples hobble, burros clip clop, children screech and run in all directions. Dark-skinned men in sheep white or dirt brown jellebas, some just in limp work shirts and torn pants, sit on curbs, stairwells, against walls, anywhere there is shade, smoking. I stood out, struggling through the dank alleys, crossing the burning boulevards, hopping the grease-grimed cobblestones of the city streets, like the exotic animal I was.

A monkey loose in the streets of Tangiers!

My escape from the ship was made good, now if I could just get through all the criss-crossing legs crowded on the street, not get overwhelmed and die of curiosity and strange sights, and not get caught by the hands that jumped clawing out of the crowd at me, the feet that kicked at me, the calls of interest and surprise. As I hastily made my way up the steep streets, slid at full run around corners, I was constantly spotted and pursued. I was getting tired just hustling out of reach of a curious and bored populace that wanted to capture me for their own unknown reasons.

There were many beautiful sights that I wanted to investigate when I felt safe. The tall houses, piled on top of one another going up the hillside reminded me a bit of Arkteepa's temple. I saw piles of fruit and food. I could smell real monkey treats, oranges, onions, and spices everywhere. But I didn't know where I was going, I didn't know where protection lay. So I had to do some fast learning. If I got tired and stopped, something would catch me.

So I kept moving. Trotting up alleys, scurrying along side streets, I climbed higher into the surrounding walled fortress of the Kasbah. I was now near the top where garden courtyards hid behind walls and a few auburn palms trunks, elephantine and slouching, grew up out of the sidewalks. I came to a courtyard wall hung with carpets of orange flowering marguerite and red hibiscus draped low over its sides. I quickly climbed this viney hedge, leapt from the wall to a ragged palm ascending like an elevator on high, and climbed up the fifty feet to the top.

There I found a safe spot, clung to that tree, and slept.

Chapter 33

I awoke that evening the starving animal that I was. I looked out from my treetop over the crowded city of Tangiers.

The evening sun was making its warm sweep across the square rooftops of the city. I could see women in kerchiefs standing on their roofs at clothes lines tending washed clothing, strings of dried peppers, sheep skins, colored rugs hung on the lines like unreadable messages made with flags between ships. Other women sat on mats sorting or cutting food in buckets and bowls. Distant street sounds rose to my ears, honks, shouts, tinny meowing music. Below me, the streets were still full of milling people. Veiled and hooded women in heavy-hipped robes lumbered along sidewalks like cows. Men in skull caps prodded heavily burdened donkeys with sticks into brisk walks down alley ways past children kicking cans and plastic bottles as toys. Above the streets, large black swallows were turning busily in the air like bees suddenly released from their hive, swooping for insects just above the heads of the unseeing pedestrians. Still sodden with the darkness and isolation of the ship, I looked on with awe. It was wonderful to see the activity. I lifted my nose for scents. The air was musty with the smell of dinner smoke.

I was a monkey high and alone over a bustling city. I was one hungry monkey. And I wasn't sure if I dared go down there to eat.

It was a beautiful and interesting place. And any fool hopper could see it was dangerous.

The orange sun was setting amber in the West. Then as the shining ball descended at the horizon and shadows flooded the city hillside, I heard something from a distant tower. Coming from high over the Arab medina across from my perch, I heard the voice of an old man call out to his people.

"Aaaaaaaallllaaaah huuuuuuaaaa Kaaabar Min kulllliiiiii Wahed!"

It was a slow melodious call. A relaxed call to the people below from a high mosque tower. The activity in the city streets slowed a beat. No car horns honked. And again that tremulous voice of an elder, rasping and wavering, called out.

"Allah hua kabar min kulli wahed!"

"God is greater than everyone of us!"

This song reminded me of the jungle, reminded me of the sad song of the Great Lily, reminded me of the evening calls rockthrowers sing from the top stones of Arkteepa. A long call of sadness. A long call back to the community. A lone call at the end of the day of remembering who you are. This evening prayer sung out over the city was somehow a comfort to me, a beauty, something familiar and soothing in a foreign land. Here was a people who also called out to the tribe.

And though it was a strange populace, a strange land, I felt at home for hearing it.

Chapter 34

"Who are you?"

I nearly didn't understand the words, they were so different from mine. I looked at her, a feminine monk, gingery red, nearly blond from the Berber mountains. An attractive graceful female. I felt an immediate interest in her, surrounded in the setting of her cage. What should I answer her? Would she understand what I said? And who was I? I was a rockthrower, but really more than that, I didn't have the language to say, even if I knew the answer.

"What is your name?" were my first words to her. Somewhere in the background noise of the Kasbah, I heard a donkey braying in laughter.

"Kory," was her reply.

She had now stood up on the wooden floor of her cage and walked to the bars, pushing her cute nose at me. Her eyes carried a certain hopeful curiosity. Years later, as I grew used to the zoo, I recognized it was the animals who had this hopeful curiosity as they lived in their cages that did best in the zoo. They learned more and their keepers were happy to see them. Kory, a thin and pert berber monkey, with high almost feline cheekbones, sat looking at me, a strange brown monkey dropped out of the briar hedge, packed thick as library books, that surrounded her courtyard cage.

I had discovered her in the Kasbah during one of my evening escapades to snag food. I had haunted the Kasbah, its dark alleys, its eerie vegetation that grew up free and wild in the Arab city for two weeks now. I had learned to shamble the side streets like a cat, head down, so that a disinterested glance saw only another alley animal, nothing unusual, though if one looked close it was easy to see my tail was a half foot too long and my ears too round to be a Moroccan alley cat. So I had learned to get about in the early dawns and dimming evenings without too much street hassle. Food was everywhere. I was fast adapting to my new surroundings.

Children, of course, with their innately clear and youthful vision, saw I was a monkey immediately. They never mistook me for a lanky cat, even in the bad light. Thus, I would be spotted as I sneaked behind garbage cans, shinnied up drain pipes, leapt the stone doorsteps and the charge was on. Whoops! I would try to look smaller and run. I'd dart for escape, any kind of cover, as a pack of clopping children's feet came running after me in the medina. A strange animal in a land where he didn't belong. Happy and bloodthirsty children pursing me!

I had to take great caution not to get cornered.

"Are you a monkey like me?" asked Kory.

I blinked and nodded. Of course, we were nearly identical except for our fur. She was a caged monkey, me a monkey in the wrong land. I later realized that she had probably been taken from her family as I had, perhaps so long ago, that she didn't recognized other monkeys like herself. This was a young female who'd spent a long time being isolated and alone, her monkey nature misunderstood by her keepers and thus, mistreated.

"Do you want out?" I asked. I had been a monkey alone now for many weeks since my capture. I wanted this other animal out and beside me.

She sat in her cage looking at me as if she didn't comprehend.

Finally, she nodded that she did want to escape.

She said that was all that she really wanted.

She backed away to the rear of the cage as if frightened as I worked my monkey fingers at the twine knotted beneath the cage that held the door shut. I was breathing quickly trying to get the cage door untied. I wanted her out, perhaps more than she wanted out herself. She remained in the back of the dark cage, watching me work at the door. It was as if she thought I wanted into the cage to take something from her.

All I wanted was someone out with me.

Finally I chewed the knot off the twine and with several stiff jerks pulled the hutch door open.

"Come out," I said jumping back down on the ground beside the cage.

With the door open wide, I saw no movement in the dark cubicle. I sat for a minute. There was still no movement. I had expected this female to come scrambling out in earnest. But to my surprise, it was now quiet and still in the cage where she hid.

I backed off into the courtyard, farther toward the briar hedge and the palm tree I had picked out to climb for escape.

Why wasn't she coming out? I realized that she must have been in that cage so long that the sight of escape and freedom was too daunting for her to dare.

It was then a lone old dog woofed in the far corner of a courtyard. It was the raspy woof of a mutt, penned away in a shed, unable to get out. It had awaken with the smell of my monkey scent. Alone and unable to get out, the Arab cur was pacing about, woofing through the split cracks in the wooden shed door.

I hastened to the foot of the palm tree. Then I stopped and looked back.

The cage door was still black and open. No sign of life.

As I sat at the base of the palm, wondering about this female monk's hesitation, the old dog caught sight of me through the shed door. This set off quite a racket, the penned dog growling and howling in its lonely shelter.

Now I could hear Arab voices muttering through one of the open windows overhead. The dog continued to bugle.

Footsteps were padding down verandah stairs. I could see an Arab man, mustached and unsmiling, descending to the courtyard carrying a stick.

I could wait no longer, I had to climb the tree to escape discovery.

I turned to go.

"Wait! Wait for me!"

Kory had seen me leaving. And now, in desperation, she knew it was now or never.

A black shadow sprang out the cage door, even as the Arab man raised his stick and exclaimed with surprise, seeing Kory's escape.

I stopped and the other fleeing monkey shot past me and scrambled up the tree, her tail held high.

Fleeing the barking dog and calling Arab, I followed her up into the dark.

We jumped from the palm onto a nearby courtyard wall, climbed a drain pipe, and crossed many rooftops in our escape.

As I followed her jogging and leaping over the medina, I found she had a sweet milky scent that I had never known.

Chapter 35

It's now that I realize I fell in love with her instantly.

Chapter 36

Kory was a beautiful monkey. In my initial days with her, I was immediately taken by her. Her face was graceful, high in the cheeks and long in the nose. A lovely, nearly feline monkey face. She had a lithe body, very female in her carriage and walk. I enjoyed just being in her presence.

It was later, as I spent more time with her wandering the medina at night and dawns, like every monkey working for its living, that I discovered Kory was a monkey of hidden talents. In her long confinement in the backyard cage, years of being sternly monitored, pestered, erratically fed by her keepers, she had developed strong skills for living, managing sparse food, defending herself by foreseeing, and wearing the camouflage of sociability before her captors to ensure food, water, and some small comfort. Before her captors, in her cage, she lived in a kind of misunderstood fear, an uneasiness, that stole security from her, even though her cage had been secure. She was an uneasy monkey, and so to survive she adapted to win what warmth, comfort, shelter that she could, and she won it. As best any caged monkey could.

But she remained a monkey alone in a cage, which leaves what could be a robust, excited monkey heart half-filled, waiting. Isolated. Which I supposed explained why, when we walked together, she walked close. Although I was a monkey from a different tribe, I was at least a monkey. A tall monkey, and so perhaps acceptable to her as something of a wall, a barrier of protection beside her, that was perhaps something like a wall of her cage.

Within the first evening of prowling for food, I learned that Kory spoke cat. Excellent cat. She also spoke a little dog. Her main visitors from the courtyard that held her cage. She also understood rat, but wouldn't speak a word of it.

I first discovered her language talents when we were walking down an alley one night looking for food. She suddenly began walking in swaying, arched curves, twitching her tail, and making mewing noises. A scruffy black tom cat that was reservedly treading the opposite side of the cobblestone alley stopped and looked over at us. Kory made several soft meows.

The Moroccan tom meowed back.

"What are you doing?" I asked surprised.

"I'm asking where to go for food," she said.

I sat down amazed as she and the tom meowed several more times to each other. Then the black cat, tail in air, quickly strutted off down the alley and out of sight.

"You speak cat?" I asked.

"Yes."

"And he told you where to find food?" I asked.

"Well, not exactly. I speak cat well enough that in the dark they can't tell I'm a monkey, so he was willing to talk. Those Tom's are always on the lookout for any excuse to talk to a female. But alley cats, no thanks." Kory gave a little shiver to signify repulsion at the species.

"But when I started asking about foods, vegetables and fruity garbage, things that cats don't eat, he got suspicious. I expect he looked closer, then took off in a huff. He'd only talked to me because he thought he could exploit me. Then he saw he couldn't exploit me, so he left."

"Exploit you?"

Kory looked at me a shaded glance, "in a rutting-way." Kory laughed, "Cats! Once he realized his mistake, all he could believe was that now I was going to exploit him somehow! Narrow-minded ignoramus. He couldn't get what he wanted, and so he left before I could exploit him. All he could see was himself."

"Where did you learn cat?"

"The cage," Kory shrugged.

"Why?" I asked.

"I guess in hopes of escaping the cage. The need to talk with somebody. Anybody..." Kory shrugged again so deeply that I realized the depth of isolation she had experience for years.

"I even learned dog," admitted Kory.

"Oh? I said.

"Yeah, late at night, when the dog was in the shed, I would woof and tell him some steak was just outside his door. It drove him crazy," Kory smiled. "He'd get furious and then bang against the door, woofing. The whole house would wake up, and the man would come down and give that old woofer hell."

Kory laughed.

"What's so funny?" I asked.

"Once I did it every night for a week. That dog was so dumb. His Arab master had to come down and give it to him every night!"

Kory laughed again at how horrid she had been. I saw there was a black cutting edge to Kory's humor, laughing at the stupid pain befallen this doggy churl. When Kory looked at my face and saw my raised eyebrow and questioningly look, she burst into hysterical laughter.

"You must have been in that cage a long time," I said.

wKory nodded, breathlessly.

"I was."

"You were?" I asked.

"Years," said Kory.

There was a silence between us. The idea of years captive in that cage was sinking in now, as I thought back to the box I had managed to unlatch and let her out of. It would have allowed no more that one hop of her monkey legs to cross. For a wild-hearted monkey, that was the same as a human trying to pack up his belongings and live in a shoe. Impossible.

Yet, here she was. She hadn't died in a year as I expect most young monks separated from their tribe would. So, if her humor had a streak of pain running through it, well it had its charm, it was humor anyway, and it made sense. It was pain dispossessed, an escape and defense against the current ever-present cage-pain.

"That was hard," I said in confirmation. I had tasted a little human confinement.

"What was hard?" asked Kory, misunderstanding.

"You being in the cage for years," I said.

Kory sat down and looked at me.

She nodded and looked away quickly.

"Yes," she admitted after several seconds of silence.

She swallowed slowly as she looked back down the dark alley from which we had come.

"Years," Kory said softly to herself.

Then she shrugged, looked at me, and whispered,

"I even learned rat."

Chapter 37

Today it is raining. The water seeps and runs in snail trails down the glass front of my cage. Enclosed in the monkey house, the storms and snaking winds never enter my enclosure. I'm protected by glass. The glass front that zoo-visitors stare through at me. I, who lived unprotected in the wilds of Arkteepa, the typhoon rains splashing like fire hoses against the temple stones,as my people huddled in our damp nests in the tree tops, riding in them as they swayed like the necks of giraffes at run. I, who felt the sun bake down on my back, making the dust rise like smoke if I shook myself. I, who would run drenched with dew, my fur stringy and hirsute as I leapt through the morning bushes in the first bright instants of Spring mornings. I, I am protect by glass from any short burst of fresh air.

A monkey surrounded by walls of near paranoid protection. The zoo-keepers, in their blue uniforms with the name badges on their chest, they want to keep me alive and so protect me.

Roof over my head, I'm protected from the changes in weather. Walls and glass around me, I'm enclosed and my body kept in place. They protect me from the elements I was made to live within.

And the sad fact remains.

Mainly they protect me from the people who come to the zoo.

Chapter 38

When Kory and I came to the zoo, we were separated and put in different cages. I didn't see her again for many months until I learned a thing or two about the zoo.

I thought I would never see her again. They kept my cage dark for a week to let me get used to it.

A safe new home.

All I could hear were other monkeys elsewhere in the monkey house howling and screeching in their own glass jungles. It was no prayer call to the tribe.

These were the screeches of frustration and despair.

Chapter 39

Our first few nights together, we homeless monkeys slept in an empty Moroccan classroom. School was out and the building deserted. After scrambling and galloping away across the rooftops, we crept in through the broken window of a classroom, two exhausted monkeys. The only inhabitants of the room were skittering lizards that ran in an incredible upside down waggle across the ceiling. Kory and I bedded down as best we could, shoulder to shoulder for comfort, listening to the strange night sounds of a dark freedom-filled world that was not our own.

Shoulder to shoulder, dozing in the heat, I was glad for the comfort of this other monkey. It eased my pain and feelings of separation. Yet we had nary said a word to each other since Kory's escape.

Dawn came with the rusty pumping call of guinea fowl lurking and calling in the scrub bushes around the school yard.

I awoke alert and extremely clear-headed as I jumped to the window sill and looked out on the schoolyard in the first dawn light. Kory was still asleep, her legs and arms pulled into a knot underneath her as a cat sleeps.

"Kory, I'm hungry," I said.

Kory stirred, stretched in an feline arch, and looked around her. For an instant, I saw her demeanor register an anxiousness that she was not in her cage. Her head hastily switched to each of the four corners of the classroom. Then the realization of her escape came home and she visibly relaxed.

"I'm not in the cage," she said. Then she smiled.

"No, you're not," I confirmed.

Suddenly Kory rolled on her back, kicking her feet bicycle-pedaling in the air. She screeched merrily.

Running across the room, she leapt to the window sill where I sat.

Beside me, she looked out on the empty schoolyard, the dirt court, the poorly painted ochre and tan buildings with their fractured plaster, and she saw a new world.

"Let's get out there," Kory crowed, "I'm hungry."

Chapter 40

Cafes were our favorite hunting ground. In the morning, we would haunt the alleyways behind the downtown cafes, eating the discarded croissants and pastries found there. Oddly, but as Kory and I picked at the food we found and liked, we were almost always surrounded by Moroccan cats sitting calmly in attitudes of relaxation and indifference on boxes, garbage cans, and broken chairs in the alley. They had tended to their eating needs and now could let the world go its ways. They didn't care about us. Two more animals, albeit monkeys, gathering food among them was a matter of indifference, merely a sight to be watched.

As we sat and munched flaky bread crusts or chewed the tossed out fruits, Kory and I would eventually become aware of each other as we slaked our hunger.

I realized first that we tended to stay close. Kory and I were rarely more than a few feet away from each other. I suppose it was an unconscious need for protection. We were, after all, surrounded by wild alley cats, wily and quick. Relaxed in their full-bellied composure of fed cats, they rested like stuffed animals about us, but were an unknown quantity. The cats I knew in the jungle were quick, aggressive, and deadly. They could turn on you and bring harm your way in an instant. And though these Moroccan cats did not emanate this same aggressive air, I had trouble giving up the sense of danger from them that I had inherited from the jungle. I didn't realize that most of these lounging bodies had a fatalistic vision that we monkeys were so close in appearance to cats that there was little they could do to catch or eat us. And so they had practically no interest in us. We were mere points of interest in an eternally boring life-style. Of course, that's outside of the fierce hair-flying bloody squabbles that went on within their families and alley cat realm.

I soon found out that Kory had an uncanny ability to understand humans. Perhaps it was her long capture endured among them, but she could merely watch a human for a few minutes and know what he or she was up to. She could tell when Arab women, veiled and scuttling down the alleyways, were going to meet their secret mates. A stumbling old man in rags and dirty turban would limp into the alley and Kory, senses alert, could in a few moments tell me there was no danger for us, this man was merely looking for a place to sit and smoke his keef. Yet she once saw a clean-faced Moroccan teenager and grabbed my tail, screeching, and set us in a panic-flight out of the alley. She'd seen the black-eyes of a carnivore, a slayer. And indeed, from the safety of high tree limbs, we looked back down into the alley to see this boy catch a dog, cut its throats, and throw it quivering and spurting blood onto a trash heap. For no apparent reason! It was just done. A walking black shadow of killing, personified in human form.

Each thing she saw and communicated to me about an approaching human became immediately true. She could tell me who was a drunk, a thief, a liar, who was stupid, cowardly, or ashamed.

Even, on one rare occasion, she was able to spot a kind human, one that bent and dropped dinner bread to us from a high balcony when we approached openly in the late evening. This an act I had been deathly afraid to perform.

Yet Kory's sense of humans was unmistaken and ever true. I soon grew use to her appraisals and accepted them without question.

On the other hand, later in the zoo, Kory always knew when she had a smiling, but secretly malicious zoo-keeper. And she knew immediately she was in for months of secret pain.

But most amazing to me was the surprising discovery of Kory's innate ability to leap. Of all her hidden talents, this was the most awe inspiring to me. Kory could leap.

Leap not just like a monkey, or rockthrower, not like a baboon, but like a jaguar! Actually she could leap higher and farther than any jaguar I had ever seen. Kory was an coiled spring that would release and she would be gone! Boing! Out of sight.

And when a rockthrower admires the leaps of another leaper, that's saying something.

On one nightly food expedition, I turned around in the alley to find Kory gone.

"Kory? Where are you?" I called.

"Here, dummy," came her patient voice from above.

I looked overhead to find Kory clinging to a balcony railing two stories overhead. Her free hand was full of peach slices that she had filched from a kitchen bowl left out on the wall.

"These are good. Here," she called swinging by one arm and dropping slices of ripe peach down into the alley to me.

I looked at the wall. It was a vertical climb without handholds twelve feet up. There was no way I could climb that high to meet her.

"How did you get up there?" I asked puzzled.

"I jumped," Kory replied.

My look of disbelief made the red monkey swinging overhead laugh.

She let go, and using the friction of the wall to brake her fall, she dropped with a thump down beside me. She hopped over to a slice of peach she had dropped and began eating it.

"You can leap up there?" I said, staring back up at the impossible height.

"Uh huh," was Kory's reply as she continued nibbling.

I said nothing until Kory laughed again at my disbelief.

"Here, I'll show you."

Kory walked to the base of the wall and crouched. The hair on her back arched in a feisty cockscomb and suddenly she sprang up.

Her leap shot her incredibly nearly nine feet up, at which point she planted all four feet upon the wall and leapt again. Arm outstretched, she caught the balcony rail with ease and hung relaxed some twelve feet over my head. Kory had sailed up the wall with the fast instantaneous glance of a rock skipped across water.

"See?" she called, looking back down at me. She began filching more peach slices out of the exposed bowl on the balcony wall.

I looked up at her, hanging over my head, feeling slightly left behind. I could never repeat such a leap.

And with time I learned that she could make such leaps at will. And often did. Once I saw her leap entirely over a car—lengthwise. Add to this that the car was slowly moving toward her, and it was her only escape!

A marvelous leaper. Kory was amazingly fleet. A sailing vertebrate. A simian champion of her homeland's leafy heights!

I was to eventually learn that her leaping ability often left average leapers like myself frustrated and puzzled, wondering where she was. You might think she was somewhere lagging behind, when you would turn only to find she had actually leapt far ahead. You were the slow-footed animal. It wasn't her, it was you.

Later in the zoo, I would actually see some fellow chimps and bumble-handed orangutans refuse to believe she had this leaping ability. Even when they saw it with their own eyes. They could not accept that this furry, feline little package had so much more grace and power in her leaps than they. They denied she had any leaping ability at all. Instantly turning themselves into fools as far as I was concerned. But then, zoo animals, they become more lame-headed and stupid if so inclined.

The jungle has a way of dealing with the lame-headed and stupid. Eventual, inevitable, and ineluctably final.

And zoos don't.

But there was no doubt, Kory was a marvel.

Chapter 41

After foraging for our food in the cool deserted hours of the morning, Kory and I repaired to our lair to wait out the heat of the day. After several days hiding in the school room, we found a more convenient nesting ground in the balcony of a vacant apartment. The apartment was over a bar, restless with Arabs and Europeans sitting at outdoor tables on the sidewalk and walking continually in and out the open bar door like bees in a hive. Above this constant activity was the quiet and shade of a walled balcony with several boxes that were the size of monkey nests and comfy.

We could reach the apartment balcony easily from the rooftops, and it was walled off and protected from prying views on three sides. Yet, to our pleasure, we could sit upon the balcony railing, unseen, watching the goings on of the city below.

We spent many hours during the heat of the day lounging and preening on the balcony. In the early evenings, as the city of Tangiers came out to promenade on the sidewalks, we watched the milling people, the pushcarts moved trudging through crowds, the honking taxis, the vendors calling like roosters. Ours was a view of a free-form, relaxing zoo. Quite a spectacle for two monkeys, one from the jungle, one fresh from a cage.

I remember one hot morning, Kory had snatched a large chunk of watermelon and hauled it to this home away from home. We two had sat slurping watermelon, chewing down to the green rind, as the African heat had passed over the city like an iron flattening the street activity with its heat. The whole day we did nothing but munch watermelon and watch the occasional moped rider, bicyclist, or hobbling pedestrian, cumbered in the heavy Arab garments, forced to cross the white-hot city boulevards.

During these hours, Kory and I had a lot of time to talk. Slowly I learned what her captured life had been like.

I learned surprisingly that she referred to her captors as her family!

"What was it like? Were you always in the cage?" I asked.

"No," replied Kory, inspecting her tail, "often I was taken into my family's house. I was something of a pet for the woman. They had a son, but he had no real interest in me. He was the pride of this Arab family. I was something to supply him entertainment, trained to bring fruit, dates, and things to him when he called for them."

"A Keeper," I said.

Kory nodded. "A boy's monkey Keeper." Kory made a glum expression. "But, in truth, I was the woman's pet. She focused her..." Kory hesitated, as if pained by something in her stomach, "attentions on me."

I was soon to learn what these attentions meant.

The Arab man of this household was small of posture, but keen minded, and cobbled shoes first in the Medina, but later, as his success grew, he had opened a new shop in the New City, a shop with a window that showed European shoes. His wife, however, remained sequestered in the home. She was not happy to be home alone, and she was often nervous and unsatisfied. Alone in this Arab house for many hours, she was edgy and critical. Kory became the focus of this unhappiness.

The woman would bring Kory into the house to be a companion, but an unhappy animal companion that this woman could focus her frustrations upon, precisely because Kory was an animal. Dependent, captive, and subject to her critical discipline, Kory was let wander freely about the house. But at any instant, this woman might unexpectedly approach Kory, quietly feeding on a table, and scream with rage and chase her from the room. The frustration exploded on Kory somewhat at random, so that it was hard to learn the rules. Kory might nap upon a pillow one day and be chased angrily from it the next. In truth, it made no difference. Over several years, Kory learned to always expect angry rebukes as the result of any innocent monkey activity. Her days and months spent in the house were filled with uncertainty, such that Kory always kept a distance from the woman. Yet, sooner or later, the woman always found reason to give chase to Kory, sending her skittering for her life, running about the four corners of the house.

And a captive monkey in a house cannot ever get away. Kory's relationship with her was one of tolerance, distance, and expected abuse. I could see, as Kory told me these things, that she maintained a mighty demeanor of not caring about this woman or what living in the household had been like.

I was aghast that there seemed to be no affection for a cute monkey pet in this Arab household at all. It must have been a cold place.

Like living among the snow monkeys.

Chapter 42

Kory's torment at the hands of the Arab wife continued over a great deal of her young life. And so, in the name of endurance, she grew used to wearing the camouflage of an uncaring attitude, uncaring about oneself in the face of unavoidable, unfair pain, such that she had a shy and still courageous demeanor. Yet, as she talked to me one day of the woman's antics towards her, I could see the long unattended pain rising, then a look of disbelief and depression filled her monkey being.

We had been sitting on the balcony watching the city below when I saw this change in her.

"What's wrong?" I asked.

Kory shrugged and pointed to a telephone pole some fifteen feet from the balcony ledge.

"I could jump to that," she said. Then she was silent.

I cocked my head and scratched my chin, trying to penetrate why Kory was so glum.

"So?" I said. "I couldn't," I admitted, "It's too far. Why aren't you happy that you could make that leap if you needed?"

Kory made a face of great distaste, the same face rockthrowers make when we spot baboons in the carnal act, and she shook her head as if to shed cold water.

"What is it, Kory?" I coaxed.

"It's that woman, something she did once," said Kory.

"What?" I said, "Did she hit or hurt you or something?"

"No." Kory shrugged.

"One day I had been having a good day. I had been taken into the house, and it was quiet, and there was fruit and vegetables all about. It was the days of fasting and feasting during Ramadan. I was sampling fruits and dates all during the day. The woman, she had remained sitting nearly motionless in the kitchen, fasting. I remember her sitting there." Kory shivered.

"She was still, grey as a statue. I had watched her from time to time feeling uneasy, yet the fruits and feast-day treats were too much to pass up. I didn't hide away, as my intuition told me."

"Then finally, at sunset, I heard the prayer call that tells when the fasting ends and the feasting begins. The long call from the mosque tower hung long in the air, and then subsided."

"The house was still empty. The Arab man had not returned for the Ramadan feast, the fruits, bake goods, and soup the wife had prepared for him. Nor had the son come home. Except for the wife and I, the house was empty."

"It was time to feast, but the woman was alone."

"Suddenly, she stood in the kitchen and looked about. Her eyes fell on me, nibbling a slice of orange under the table. I could see her anger charge her face. But it was a horrid and brutal anger, more than what I normally saw."

Kory stopped a moment and swallowed painfully.

"Yes?" I said.

"I felt that day was the day she was really to going hurt me. I dropped the orange peel with a shriek as she lunged and picked up a hot frying pan from the stove. I ran form the room with her giving chase."

"I ran from one room to another, screeching and leaping over chairs, tables, and pillows. The woman's face was filled with rage, yet she pursued me in utter silence. She walked after me with calm stalking patience."

"I ran upstairs to the highest rooms. I headed to a third story room with a door to a small balcony that overlooked the street. It was the boy's room where he kept his clothes, belongings, and sleeping mat. I had always taken care to never enter this room. For to break something here, I knew my life would be in danger."

"But now I was desperate, I could hear the woman plodding heavily up the stairs following me."

"I ran into the boy's room. The door to the little balcony was open. I skittered out and jumped up on the balcony ledge. It was three-stories up, and the possibility of a fall was fearsome. But, there, just beyond the balcony was a palm. It was just a little bit farther from the balcony than that pole," said Kory with a nod toward the pole before us now.

"I decided that if the woman came onto the balcony, no matter what, I would jump. I prepared myself for my longest leap."

"And what happened?" I said, uneasy.

"When the woman walked into the room, pan raised, hunting me, she looked out and saw me crouched on the balcony. She stopped. She could see that I was ready to jump. She stopped and she stood still, watching me. "

"She stood still to let me know that I could come down off the balcony wall and run past her. I think she had realized that if I jumped, she would be truly alone. She knew that if she took another step I would fly out from the balcony into space."

"And did you jump?" I asked.

"No," said Kory. Then she burst into long lamenting sobs. Kory melted into a huddled monkey, shivering and crying. I watched, not knowing what to do or say, as this female cried uncontrollably.

"Why are you crying, Kory?" I asked softly, "You made the decision you had to. You didn't leap to your death. It's a good choice not to die when there's no chance to reach freedom."

Kory's mouth was open, showing her sharp monkey canines, her eyes squinted shut in tears. She shook her head in misery.

"No, no, that's not the pain," cried Kory, shaking her head. Then she looked at me through watery eyes.

"You see, I knew I could have made that leap."

Chapter 43

At a critical moment, in fear, Kory had not leapt. She had not been herself and jumped from the balcony and beyond to freedom. Instead, she told me she had slunk down and scurried past the Arab woman, back downstairs to the only security and safety she knew: her cage.

I saw that the realization of this, now that we were two monkeys free to roam and pinch food wherever we wished, was a crushing pain to Kory. The false path she had taken made this past choice nearly unbearable.

Later in the zoo, I was to understand better how Kory's return to the cage was a natural choice. You see, animals that grow up in cages, in the zoo, they rarely escape. If a zookeeper accidentally leaves a door open, the next morning, the animal will usually be found still in its cage or not far off.

You see, when zoo animals think of escape, going beyond the boundaries into the unknown, its difficult for them to picture, beyond the zoo, anything other than another zoo.

Chapter 44

One of the most mistreated animals here in the zoo is Sheena, the black panther. It's because of the little known fact that black panthers snarl. Not just snarl out of anger, but snarl at all things, even things interesting, beautiful, or amazing. Panthers are the kind that snarl at their newborn young. They snarl at their fresh-downed kill. They snarl in the deep tangle of jungle runners and trees at a small window of sky framing a bright moon. Some snarls end with a hiss, others with a licking of the lips. And that makes the whole difference.

But the zookeepers don't know this. So when they approach Sheena's cage, they always bang the steel bars with a lead pipe to set her slinking back. She snarls.

They throw her dead and drooping cow meat. She snarls again.

They yell and poke her with a pole to hear her outraged snarl in return.

They shoot her with a dart and she snarls as she loses consciousness.

To receive a little kindness, she'd have to meow like a kitten or wag her tail like a foot-licking pup.

But, Sheena, the black panther, she can only snarl.

And late at night, past midnight, in the black black cages, before the zoo animals awaken for our nightly travels and exploits, at a certain instant there is a hush, a stillness in the zoo, and all the monkeys wait to hear it. Across the way in the big cat house, we all know that Sheena is asleep and dreaming.

And we hear her snarl.

Chapter 45

I have felt bad for the black panther, but not as bad as when they threw Kory's body in the garbage pit in the back of the zoo.

Then I was truly devastated.

Chapter 46

Whenever Kory cried, or in the depth of the night when we squatted chilled side-by-side, I put my monkey arm around her. But it was strange, it seemed to have no effect, as if she couldn't feel it. Such ran the depth of her uncaring.

As we went about our daily scurry for food and our leisurely preening fleas and scratching, Kory was always sociable and a pleasant being to be around. She chattered at our luck in finding good foods. She giggled if I threw our garbage rinds off the balcony onto the unsuspecting bar denizens below. She submitted to looking at the back of my neck for fleas. But there was no strong bond of caring reflected back.

She'd been a caged monkey for a long time, and suffered so many losses, that clinging to another primate for warmth, for connection to the tribe, was nearly impossible.

—Even when I was sitting there right in front of her, another monkey without a tribe, needing her as badly as I wanted her to need me.

After several weeks, we grew used to each other. We were companions.

One day, late in the afternoon, with still hours to kill before she and I could go out and search our evening meal, I was watching Kory. She was sitting across the balcony, spinning a small stone on the balcony floor like a top. She was amused by this isolated spinning that her clever paws could create.

I walked up behind her to look over her shoulder. I actually put my chin on her furry neck as I looked over at the spinning stone on the floor. It was a pale pink stone that Kory has somehow spotted and rescued from a gutter. She spun it and it clicked and hopped, a dancing entity. Kory was immersed in the activity. As I leaned over her, I could smell her fur, puffy with fresh air, and feel her warmth against my belly. I put my nose to her ear and breathed in deeply. Playfully, I chewed her neck.

Kory slowly stopped spinning the stone. Soon she was sitting motionless as I leaned over her shoulder. She looked back at me with a strange look in her eyes. A look of intense interest to see what I would do.

I chewed her neck a bit more.

Then I felt Kory, still serious, raise her rump. It pushed into my belly. This set up a deep reverberation in my body. And somehow, it was as if this was a challenge from Kory.

I mounted her and we rutted for the first time.

I, Tip, the one who calls from the highest tree, say this monkey pleasure is great. Keth, the Elephant God, and Binah, our jungle mother, invented rutting, and gave it as a gift to all the little folk, the suffering monkey tribes. It helps us quell our innate loneliness.

What a great pleasure I experienced in Kory, this red Berber monkey. And as I dismounted from her and she turned to face me, I saw in her face she had experienced this same ancient gift.

Although I had mounted other monkeys before in my youthful jungle home, I had never completed the rutting act. This was the first time that I had rutted to a luxurious completion. I believe this was the same for Kory. Separated from me, she sat a moment with her eyes closed. Then she shivered. Turning slowly to me, she said no words, but came around me and began to chew my neck.

We retired to one of the boxes that was our monkey nest and lay down to nap, —Kory's pale spinning stone resting unlooked at on the floor.

Chapter 47

I was attacked once while hunting food in the deep Medina. I was sauntering down an alley, some blocks from Kory. Moroccan cats were everywhere, lying on boxes and balcony ledges, sitting on doorsteps, all licking their paws and looking about with incredible boredom. It was early evening, but Ramadan had come, and so when the prayer call to the people of Tangiers went out, the busy streets cleared, and the city quieted, as all went home to break their fast with soup and dates. Like a tide retreated far back, the streets became empty. And we animals, Arab cats and two lone monkeys, came out early to prowl.

The sounds of drums, celebratory singing, the high howling ululations of Arab women filled the evening skies over the city. With an empty city, I was at ease probing the alley trash bins, surrounded by the cats. I hopped over to look at one promising box and retrieved a nearly whole banana, when an animal rose from behind it. I hadn't seen it as I approached, and here a growling German shepherd, its brown and nearly green coat hanging like a loose uniform, lunged forward and caught my paw in its mouth.

This was quite a surprise and I looked on at this growling beast wide-eyed. I tried, but couldn't tug my hand away. The dog had me, but it seemed somehow incapacitated, as if it were drunk or dizzy with sickness. Where I expected the animal to lurch forward for a bite, and then a hair-flying, scratching fight for my life, this ragged dog merely shook its head, my paw still in its mouth, jostling me slightly, but without upsetting my balance. This was one inept mongrel.

I didn't want to attack for fear of giving the dog the idea.

For several instants, I stood, my hand caught ridiculously in this animal's mouth like a hopper with his hand stuck in a beehive, and I looked about at the other lounging cats in the alley for help. There was a great Tom near me, and I looked at him to see if any animal allegiance, the sense of one helping another, would come into play. After all, I'd seen alley cats move in number to investigate fights before. This old Tom, in his heavy grey black coat, looked at me, my paw caught in this stupid dog's mouth, and merely looked away.

So much for animal cooperation. I was not of the same species after all, and the dog could have me, for all this Tom cared.

So I shook my arm with all my might. And my paw came loose from this growling feeble canine.

I screeched in return at this dopey enemy and then turned to hop away. As I retreated down the sidewalk, the dog rushed forward for one last nip at my heels.

But it missed and I leapt away to safety, looking back warily over my shoulder. My bitten paw was only slightly sore.

I'd been living in the city for so long, I'd forgotten about jungle surprise attacks.

I went back to the balcony to find Kory there. I told her of the attack and my escape. We both were glad and agreed that city animals were so incompetent. This dizzy-headed dog was such a bungler.

In the jungle, I should have been dead.

Chapter 48

The next evening, I was scurrying back from our evening hunt, heading down the alley behind the Post Office, when I spotted a large beetle trundling alone on the sidewalk. It moved with a wobbling walk like a miniature train chugging along. I saw this black movement in the dimming light and decided to investigate. Beetles are sometimes tasty treats. I hopped near and put my nose down an inch or two from the sidewalk to get a better look.

Then I jerked my head back.

This beetle was actually a black scorpion, the most poisonous kind, walking fiercely with claws and tail raised down the middle of the sidewalk.

I stepped back to safety. The monkey rule is: with small, mean, and nasty, always give the right of way.

Chapter 49

One hot night, we were sleeping out on the balcony. The day's heat was holding over the city like an umbrella, and it was too hot to sleep in one of the balcony boxes. Kory and I were stretched out on the cool stone floor.

Near midnight, the bats had stopped twitching through the air, the lights in the city had gone out, except for a stranded few. The dark surrounding mountains were a black perimeter, bodiless and limiting, the beginning of the forests and jungles that Kory and I were born for.

And low over a western ridge, the moon broke. It was a moon of extraordinary size, a great yellow balloon large enough to carry a man, rising in a slate blue sky. The moonlight had fallen over Kory and I like a sheet fallen from a clothesline, and I poked Kory with my elbow to rouse her. She sat up blinking, finding herself exposed, fully bathed in moonlight. Without a word, I nodded to the roof and we two monkeys climbed the drain pipe to the building top. We sat together looking at the moon.

Kory and I leaned shoulder to shoulder looking into this distant light in the sky. I watched it rise over the mountains, the Arab city, like a far unspoken message from our true jungle lives, beckoning, as Kory and I sat, huddled, surrounded by real lives in an Arab city.

I watched as Keth, the Elephant God, carried Binah, our jungle mother shining over the city. The journey of this great yellow orb was so slow, and it was a journey in which Kory and I had to put our jungle faith.

Finally I could sit by no longer.

I climbed to the highest point of the building roof.

I called, "Keth! Keth!"

"Will you be strong enough to carry our jungle mother to us?"

"Keth, be strong! Be strong!"

"We monkey people await her."

I'm sure my lone monkey screeches were merely another animal noise over the slumbering human city.

But when I returned, I saw Kory had been crying.

Chapter 50

"What is that?" Kory said, stopping and wrinkling her nose in distaste.

We had been prancing across a nearby rooftop returning to our balcony home.

I stopped and put my nose up in the air.

The odor was unmistakable.

"Something dead," I said looking about me. "Nearby, I don't see it."

I thought perhaps a cat had fallen from a roof and died and was rotting on lower roof tiles somewhere. But there was no exposed carcass anywhere to be seen.

Kory took a step in the direction of the scent, then shook her head as if to shake the foul odor from her nose.

A window was open on the wall next to us, leading into an apartment on the next building.

"It's from there," said Kory, pointing to the black window.

She walked over to the wall and sprang up to perch on the window sill. She bent in the window to look in.

I hopped to the base of the wall, waiting to hear what she saw.

But instead of calling down to me, Kory sprang in a great leap back down from the window and charged away toward our balcony home like a cat in panic.

"Kory?" I shouted to the empty rooftop. In an instant, I had been left alone.

I looked up at the window. I determined that I could spring up there myself.

I hunched and launched myself up the wall, grasped the window ledge, and hauled myself up. As I stood at the black opening of the window, the scent of putrefaction was tremendous.

Squinting, I peeked in the window.

It was a human bathroom, complete with sink, bidet, and bathtub. In the bathtub was a swarming mound. Aghast, I looked again to see it was a human body, on its back in the bathtub, wearing a writhing cloth of flies, wasps, and vermin. Books were scattered on the floor and one school text was fallen in the tub, its pages dry, but misshapen as malformed insect wings.

I guessed this had probably been a teacher.

She had died, asphyxiated by the gas waterheater left running as she bathed. And no one had come or found her now apparently for weeks.

I felt my gorge rise. My stomach lifted to tip out my food.

A teacher, alone in Morocco, overcome, helpless, and dead in her apartment. She probably wouldn't be missed until the school year started again in the fall.

I leapt down. I ran, following Kory's path of flight, racing to get into fresh air.

Years later, alone in the zoo, I wondered if this death had been a suicide.

I decided not.

Zoo animals rarely rarely do that.

Chapter 51

Although Tangiers was a beautiful city, with free-pickings of many monkey delights, eventually my frustrations built up with living always on display among the Arab cats and the continual struggle with differences between jungle life and that of the city. Kory and I decided we would try to go home, try to make it back to her mountain forests.

Over the next week, the smell of the dead teacher grew worse. Kory and I sat on the balcony grimacing in futility. It was as if this teacher were giving us a test that none could pass other than through sheer endurance. A test in which the students were meant to fail.

Finally, Kory and I could stand it no longer and we made plans to escape the city. We were not sure where to go, or what we would do. We just hoped to get back to a forest setting where we were animals fit to live our monkey dreams.

Kory did not think the mountains that were in sight beyond the city were her mountains. So we had to prepare ourselves for a journey that might be long.

We were about to become homeless again.

Chapter 52

"Where are we?" Kory asked.

As I hopped up on the ledge of a windowed building, I wasn't sure. We had entered the grounds of a school or campus, after scrambling across the deep city, through a region of run down homes inhabited by black humans on the city's edge, and then entered an oasis of sidewalks, dried grass, palm trees, and academic buildings. It was like an island of cultured buildings surrounded by a low desert of city dwellers.

We had left our balcony home in deep night and secretly picked our way down many dark alleys looking for a way out of the city. It was dawn, with a flat sun rising on the horizon like a fried egg, when we had reached a cement entryway and barred gate.

Kory's good brains had quickly found an entrance into the school grounds.

"I'm not sure where we are," I said looking around uneasily. "It seems to be a school."

The place seemed abandoned. No humans haunted the sidewalk at this early time, no grounds keepers were watering the greenery, the Arab students had not come in yet from their country homes to continue their study in this foreign campus.

"This seems safe enough. Maybe we should find a place to hide here during the day," said Kory.

I thought this a good idea.

"Let's try there," said Kory, pointing up at the side of a building with many low balconies and windows. I looked and saw a window that had been left open several inches. Just wide enough for a wandering monkey to squeeze through.

In a single leap, Kory flew up to this new balcony and was soon beckoning me to follow.

I found a low tree and scrambled up until I could jump to the ledge where Kory sat. We both looked at the window, listening with jungle wariness. A strange scent came from the opening, but there was no movement from within.

Kory leapt to the window, squeezed in, and disappeared.

I looked back and around to make sure we were not being followed by any Moroccan denizens, then jumped and squeezed in through the window myself.

"Kory?" I said as I dropped through the window to the floor. My eyes had not grown accustom to the dim light and I couldn't see her.

"What is this place?" whispered Kory. There was an edge of amazement and distaste in her voice that set me instantly alert.

I quickly began squinting around in the dark to ascertain our surroundings.

It was a large room completely walled with high shelves. Each shelve held a militia of clear jars, each jar standing at attention with a white label on its stomach. Row after row of these large jars, the size of a tiger belly, filled the room. Isolated in the room's middle were four heavy black tables, each table with a sink and faucet set in its top. Many jars and beakers were scattered hear and there on the tables.

The air was damp and reeked with chemicals. I was filled with a low sense of disgust.

Kory was now wandering about the room, educating herself about its contents.

I sat, getting used to these strange surroundings.

After several minutes, Kory came back to me after her inspection.

"What's in all the jars?" I said, pointing at the shelves of large containers filled with a clear liquid and other objects.

"Animals," said Kory, "And parts of animals."

Kory and I sat looking around at the walls of jars holding dead animals and their parts, grimacing.

"Yuck," was Kory's final comment.

Chapter 53

We had been sitting in this glass laden room for several hours waiting for the dark to come, when Kory jumped up on one of the central black tables. I knew she was poking around among the beakers and glass tubes up there for water.

"It's dripping. There's water in this sink!" called Kory to me. As she turned my way, her long tail tipped over a rack of test tubes and they spilled like bouncing bones onto the table and shattering on the floor.

We both looked a moment at the smashed glass, but we were thirsty, and so I jumped to the table top and joined Kory there. We put our heads down into the large black ceramic sink, lapping at a shallow surface of water that meagerly entered there from a slow dripping faucet.

We had been lapping away like cats for several minutes, when we felt the air change behind us.

Then a black net slapped down over us. It as a long-handled butterfly net with a hoop of clinging black mesh.

Startled, Kory leapt straight up to escape, but the net battered her down. We fought and chewed the net, but this was useless. We found ourselves captured.

Something clicked and the room filled with light.

Kory and I crouched lower, hiding in the small cover of the laboratory sink.

I could hear a human voice speaking, excited, in tones edged with satisfaction.

A heavily gloved hand came down into the sink and we were grabbed and wrapped up into the netting.

"Tip!" cried Kory.

I was struggling in silence to get out. But the more Kory and I struggled and fought, dangling in a moving net, the more we found ourselves only struggling with each other. The man in white lab coat, still wearing the thick gloves, walked us into another room with Kory and I still shoveled up in his net.

There we were dropped like a couple of furry coconuts through a hole in the top of into a large metal cage.

Then the gloved hand descended into the cage again. It caught Kory by the tail. She screeched angrily as she was pulled back up out of the cage, and I could see her eyes were wide, looking about for any means to save herself.

Kory was dropped by the white-coated man into another identical cage next to mine.

Kory and I were again caught and held in separate cages.

Chapter 54

Kory and I sat in the cages for several days, glum and hump-shouldered like heaps of elephant dung. Each day the white-coated Arab came to look at us, offering small tins of water and the butts of lettuce and cabbages. The Arab spoke to us as he offered this food.

"What is this Moroccan human saying?" I asked, knowing Kory had some facility with foreign languages.

"He's not Moroccan. His Arabic is strange, I think he is an Algerian doctor," said Kory.

"What does he want with us?" I said.

Kory looked about the great room of labeled jars on all sides of us and shivered.

"He keeps calling us 'his little experiment,'" said Kory.

I looked at Kory with a sick feeling in my stomach.

The days passed into weeks. Kory and I sat in our little cages. We would look at each other, we would talk. But we had hardly the connection, the substance of the tribe to support us. Each day we were looked at by the Algerian doctor. Other people bustled into the room and out, some carrying brooms, boxes, some carrying dangling animals. Any animal that was brought in appeared sick. I saw a white rabbit carried in like a limp gym sock. The doctor's assistant held out the rabbit to the doctor who took it and placed it in on a wooden board. The rabbit lay still on the board, doing its fearful-rabbit thing of trying to be invisible. I watched the doctor take up a strange glass tube with a needle on the end. It looked frightening and reminded me of a snake fang. The doctor filled the instrument with a clear liquid. Then he bent over the rabbit.

The rabbit jerked and shivered.

I saw the doctor had take his needled tube and stuck it into one of the rabbit's eyes.

Chapter 55

A week later, my turn came. Each day the doctor had come in, bending over us, speaking quietly as he looked us over.

Then one day, as he approached our cages, our keen monkey eyes saw the doctor was hiding something behind his back. His hand's were gloved, and he was holding the glass syringe.

"Oh, Tip," moancd Kory.

I grimaced as the doctor stood before us. Kory had shrunk back to the farthest corner of her cage. The doctor stood staring at her.

"La belle fille, petit singette, tu a puer? N'a pas de puer," crooned the Algerian doctor, looking at poor Kory.

I began to shriek and bang about the cage.

The doctor straightened up at my commotion. He looked my way.

Then I saw him reach for the top of my cage.

His hand descended, caught my tail, and pinned my squirming body against the side of the cage nearest him. I was cawing and screeching in panic.

Then I felt a snakebite on my stomach.

When he pulled the needle from me and released me, I lay still, in shock, on the cage floor.

That was all that happened to Kory and I over the next several weeks. I had expected Kory to be attacked by the doctor at sometime as well, but this never happened. Over a long series of days, the doctor merely inspected us each day, always with the same soft words as he watched us. Each day now, another white-coated assistant stood next to him writing notes on a board.

Kory had adjusted to caged life again, but as the days passed I began to feel more and more depressed. Then I became listless, then lethargic. I had no interest in my food. I ate less and less. Finally, it worsened so that I sat for several days without moving in my cage, with a strange weight in my side. It was as if someone had sown in a stone where my liver should have been. As the doctor looked at me and nodded, the assistant nodding as well as he wrote his notes, I neither looked up nor moved. I felt too nauseous.

Kory, wearing an ever grimmer expression, watched me fading, helpless, yet churning in her cage for something to do. She told me my face had changed color, the color of rotting pumpkin.

One day, I woke up, shivering and panting. It was all I could do, grimacing with eyes shut.

"Tip? Tip?" called Kory to me. But her's was a voice that seemed far away.

I'm sure she was afraid I was about to die.

Chapter 56

That day, when the doctor inspected me, he changed my diet. From then on, all that was put in my cage were wedges of orange in the peel.

Without water or food, I was obliged to suck on them as my only sustenance.

Each day my condition worsened. I moved less, I ate less. My sickness increased. Kory was forced to watch my decline, healthy and alone in the next cage. Each day the doctor arrived, placing more wedges of orange in my cage, even though many of them had begun to pile up in the corner uneaten.

The doctor and his assistant continued to take notes of my condition. It seemed that they were merely observing me, rather than helping, with the exception of offering me more fresh oranges each day. Boxed in and sick, I felt they owned my life. But they were distant, as if they didn't care.

And of course, caring is one of the strongest medicines in the world.

But Kory, also boxed in and separated in her cage, could only struggle to give that essential medicine to me from a fearful distance. I could read on her face the helplessness, the fear that if I died she would have to cope with all totally alone.

My sickness endured and the doctor's face grew grave. I think that he hoped that my diet of oranges would somehow take effect and pull me through. Now, each day, the assistant would hold me down in the cage, stick me with a needle, and steal blood from me. This was very hard for me to sustain. My mind kept wanting to escape my body as I watched, tired and helpless, as the assistant approached with his needle and then purposefully stabbed me for my blood.

I found I had to really intensify my thoughts, keep my monkey mind focused to keep my spirit life within my body, keep it from flying out and away, during these moments of horror and lack of control.

I feared if I didn't keep my mind and spirit in my body, still under my control, I might die. I might not return to this hapless sick and orange monk lying fatigued in his cage.

Later, in the zoo, I learned not to worry about it.

Chapter 57

One night I woke in the dark. I could barely breath. My lungs were cloudy and rattling as I struggled to suck in air. It was in the deepest part of the night, Kory was asleep in the next cage, and I was tired and suffocating. I struggled to sit upright, my chest bellowing. I didn't want to wake up Kory because there was nothing she could do. I didn't want her to sit and watch me suffer. It was here, alone in the blackness, that I knew, if I was to live, I had to take care of myself. It was my decision. And as from a great distance I felt my monkey resourcefulness come back to me. I dragged myself over to the pile of uneaten orange wedges in the corner of my cage. Once near them, I bent my head over them and breathed deeply. Then I ate them, every one, peel and all.

Exhausted, I lay down and slept.

Chapter 58

The next day, I awoke groggily. The door to the laboratory had opened and the light come on. It was the Algerian doctor, entering with grim look on his face.

His assistant with his notes and clipboard were nowhere in sight.

Kory sat up as the doctor entered. I raised my head to look his way.

What I saw was disturbing. The doctor was not talking to Kory in his normal coaxing voice. He stood in front of my cage and slowly shook his head. This was like a signal to me that something had ended and the results had not been good. He slowly turned his back and went to the black tables and began making preparations.

"What is he going to do now?" asked Kory, alarmed. Laying down weak, I made no sound, just shook my head that I didn't know.

Then the doctor came back to stand before my cage. He was looking directly down on my lying form, judging my condition. He held a half-filled syringe in his hand.

Kory's jungle intuition must have told her that this syringe meant death.

She stood up and began to chatter and screech at the Algerian doctor. She jumped about and screeched so loud the doctor was obliged to face her. He began talking to calm her.

"Tu vois, your little friend is very sick. He's going to die. Petit singette, don't make so much noise. We must put him out of his misery. He can't last much longer.

Alors, it's better to make a quick end of him now," the Doctor crooned at the upset primate in the next cage.

But Kory could see what needed to be done. And she did this with all her monkey heart. She barked and chattered with renewed energy, pleading for the doctor to see me and spare my life.

The doctor began to look on at Kory with a strange half-smile.

He shook his head. "You are very wise, singette. You know what's happening. And you won't have any of it. Brave singette. You don't want to be alone. C'est ca?" spoke the doctor.

I slowly sat up, sick and shivering, so that at least the doctor could see I was sitting.

Kory continued to rant and chatter for all she was worth.

The doctor looked at me, shrugged, then lowered his syringe.

He turned away and went back to his black lab table.

Kory had saved my life.

Chapter 59

The next day I felt a little better. And a little better the day after that. I continued to eat the oranges, and now the doctor began to place other vegetables in my cage as well. Kory, who had taken to pacing her cage nervously, began to sit more. After a week, I was sitting up in my cage as well.

Kory told me my orange color was changing. I was fading fast. Soon, I hoped just to have my same old brown monkey face.

At dawn, I would wake up. I would go over to the far edge of the cage and lean against the wire. Kory would wake and lean against her cage next to mine. We were close enough that I could feel her body heat radiating toward mine. Two lone monkeys, trapped in a shelved room, lined with jars of dead and defeated animals, we leaned toward each other for the slightest comfort of the tribe. We were like two magnets, held apart, attracting one another.

The Algerian doctor came in each day and inspected me. He looked on me more relaxed, and occasionally spoke a kind word or two my way. It was only once a week now that the assistant stabbed me for blood. Less pestered by people in white coats, I felt freer, even in this cage, and so I began to feel renewed interest in life.

Unfortunately, this meant that Kory and I watched the daily activities of the lab, during which we saw some rude experiments on animals going on. Rabbits mostly.

We felt sorry for them.

Chapter 60

One day the doctor came in smiling. He looked at us, holding two sheets of paper, and money in his hand. He bent over Kory speaking softly, in pleasant tones.

"What's he saying?" I asked.

"Now that you're better, he's sold us," said Kory. "Another man has purchased us, is creating false papers, and we're going to an American zoo."

"What's a zoo?" I asked.

Kory shrugged.

"Do you think it's like a big temple?" I asked, my heart leaping toward my homeland and Arkteepa.

Again Kory shook her head that she didn't know.

Later that day, blankets were thrown over our cages. And we felt ourselves be picked up and begin moving through the air.

"Kory?" I called through the dark blanket, "Are you still there?"

"Yes," came her reply from somewhere ahead of me. Her voice was distant and calm.

Although I couldn't see her or be near her, at least I had the reassurance that we were traveling together.

Two nervous monkeys were loaded on an airplane and left Africa.

☆☆☆ The Zoo

Chapter 61

"There's a mirror in the zoo."

Jacko, the elder sage of the primates, an old orangutan with orange fur that hung from him like moss, had spoken gravely.

He looked about at each of us with his penetrating black eyes. This news was so upsetting that few of us other monkeys could return his gaze.

We sat in the cage and looked down on Caina, the mother hyena, now a still body on her concrete cage floor, grinning in near-death.

Being still new to the zoo, I didn't know what this exactly meant.

"Is she dead?" I asked.

"No. But she will be so in short span," grunted Jacko. He worked his lips in rippling distaste. Then he looked again at each one of the monks about him in the hyena cage.

"And it means that we are all in danger."

Chapter 62

"But the hyena isn't dead, won't she just wake and get up?" I asked.

"No, she won't wake. And she won't get up. Not until this mirror is broken," said Jacko to me. He could see I was puzzled. There was some kind of victim here before me in this hyena cage, yet I didn't understand.

"It is the power of the mirror. It holds her astral body paralyzed. So her corporeal body sleeps, cannot wake up. And so she will sleep until she dies," said Jacko. Again he worked his mouth like a human chewing tobacco, a sign of great distaste among orangutans.

The other primates about me were now crouched and huddled. They stared at Caina's still body, alive, yet dying, keeping silent. Their knowledge of the present danger had waken their monkey instinct for silence and stealth.

"What has a mirror got to do with it?" I asked.

Jacko turned to me with raised eyebrows and appraising eyes. "Newcomer, you've never seen the ill caused by a mirror in this zoo. But we who have, we know the horror that a mirror can produce. When a visitor forgets and leaves a mirror in the zoo, and the wrong paws find it, it becomes a powerful weapon. One that is eventually turned against us all. It is a paralyzer of astral bodies and a slayer of corporeal ones."

"A mirror is deadly in the zoo?" I asked mystified.

Several of the surrounding monkeys were now slipping through the walls to return worried to their mates. Their astral bodies simply leapt and disappeared through the man-made walls as they left.

"A mirror in the zoo deadly?" replied Jacko, grunting in ill-humor, "It is the worst weapon that can be found in the zoo."

"Who has this weapon?" I asked, still bewildered.

Jacko's lips rippled again in disgust. Then he looked at me. He paused thinking before he spoke.

"I expect it's the baboons."

Chapter 63

Two weeks later, Caina's sleeping, but lifeless body was hauled from her cage and tossed into the secret garbage pit in the back of the zoo.

There she died among the rest of the refuse.

And me, I learned that a mirror is a killer of dreams and dream animals.

Chapter 64

With the astral sun shining down, illuminating all the zoo in warm and languid August light, I crossed the grassy playground and the antelope pasture. I was heading for the tall stand of Eucalyptus trees that Kory liked to spend her time in. Each night, as the astral sun rose and we zoo animals left our bodies to hunt and forage in freedom, Kory liked to feed and then repair to the high shaggy branches. Here she would mediate and look out on the peaceful, but busy landscape of the zoo.

As I worked my way across the zoo, I looked out over the grounds. The many zoo animals were grazing, playing, leaping, tussling, the lazy-handed poking about the trash containers at the concession stand. A coven of kangaroos loped in their three-point football-player's stance across the rhino meadow. A black and orange tiger, Ramar, was asleep in the shade of a flowering lilac, his relaxed form stretched out and completely filling a park bench. Howlers were swooping and hooting as they crossed the monkey highway in the trees. A great boa, thick as a man's leg, slowly wrapped around the base of a drinking fountain and hoisted himself up to drink from its eternally flowing water.

Across the well-tended park shrubbery bright butterflies and flowers combined their whites, oranges, and yellows. A three-toed sloth was slowly knocking down purple blossoms out of a jacaranda like women's handkerchiefs. Pink flamingos and marabou storks were stilt walking the sidewalks everywhere. Elephants walked among the short trees at the petting zoo, raising their trunks like a single arm to pick the elm leaves that tasted of bee's wax and lettuce.

With a courteous wariness, I sidestepped off the sidewalk. Crocodiles, with their bumpy backs, were walking in waddling Indian file down the sidewalk, heading for the cool shallows of the children's wading pool. Head back, in proud procession, their mouths were open in slight grins.

I set off again. Ahead, gibbons were picking popcorn like white insects from the sidewalk and popping them in their mouths. On high, eagles turned in the sky in circles as slow as a mixing spoon turned by a dreamer.

I hopped to a stop as I reached the leafy litter of the Eucalyptus grove. I listened all around. The sounds of the zoo filled the air with the old sounds of the jungle that I knew from Arkteepa. I heard a distant menagerie of quacks, peacock caws, hog grunts, bleats, barks, tweets, whistles, chirps of all kinds, the bellows of the fanged and clawed, the yipes of the fleet. Insects whirred in a great flowering concert in the August heat. It was summer in the zoo, the animals roving in complete liberty. It was hot and the zoo filled with bright astral light.

And it was now just past midnight.

Chapter 65

"Kory?" I called, a bit worried, as I looked up at the base of her favorite Eucalyptus tree. It was a tall tree, over a hundred feet to the top. There Kory liked to nest in a fragrant bed of leaves and twigs still sporting buttons. I hated to climb all the way up there if she wasn't in.

I saw a small rustle of shaggy leaves at the top boughs.

So I knew she was there and I started scampering from limb to limb toward the top.

When I reached the top and stood looking about Kory's empty treetop nest, I blinked and looked about disappointed.

Then an animal fell on my back and began playfully chewing the back of my neck.

"Kory!" I laughed.

Kory giggled, and with the mock growl of a predator, said into my ear, "Remember, the unwary animal is good to eat!" And then she began shaking me until I rolled onto my back and we wrestled monkey-style for a few moments.

In wrestling, Kory and I were well matched. She was laughing as we did our juggling act of laying hands and feet upon each other. Kory's eyes always lit with a fierce black determination that made me laugh. She often won because I eventually grew weak with laughter.

"Tip, you are such a rockthrower weenie," laughed Kory.

I bit her at the base of the tail to make her squawk.

"No fair! No fair! Tail biting! Ugh!" screeched Kory.

"Sorry, Kory, I thought that was my tail I was biting," I said, gleefully.

Kory, playfully incensed, leapt again to the attack, but I held her back from my chest with arms outstretched.

"Kory, I want to talk to you. Something is happening in the zoo."

"Oh, what's that?" said Kory, ceasing to struggle.

"They've found another one," I said. "Like Caina. A body sleeping to death."

"Who?" asked Kory, instantly concerned.

"The otter," I said. "They found him sleeping face down in the water in his tank."

"Oh!"

"Kory, Jacko says it's certain now. There's another mirror in the zoo."

"No," said Kory, "How can that be? Who has it? Why would they want to kill us zoo animals?"

I shrugged.

"Jacko still believes it's the baboons."

"Any proof? Has anyone seen a baboon with a mirror?" asked Kory. Her ears were wide and turned alertly toward me.

"No, no one has seen anything. But Jacko says they would keep it hidden and secret for as long as they can. Until they learn to control it."

"What does Jacko think will happen then?" asked Kory.

I hesitated a second.

"Jacko thinks it will eventually mean more deaths, many deaths, beyond what happens in the jungle."

Kory was sitting silent. Her eyes were squinting at me in concern.

I continued with the worst.

"He thinks it will eventually mean fighting."

Chapter 66

As a rockthrower, I knew something of fighting in the jungle. I knew it was the rockthrowers who stood and savagely threw rocks at the marauding baboons. I knew it was scenes full of fear, struggle, and screaming. I knew it was generally the young and innocent who were hurt, maimed, and sometimes killed.

As a rockthrower, you merely stood in your rage, threw your rocks, and did your part. A savage bringer of pain to those bloody of tooth and claw attacking your kind. It was a furious, angry activity. Though I had been a young rockthrower in battle once or twice when I left my home, I had seen my tribe engaged in it.

But Jacko had told me fighting in the zoo was different. When a mirror was found, and destruction possible, it was not single combat, animal upon animal. It was not the deathly relationship of prey and predator. When fighting came to the zoo, the mirror was inevitably turned against entire tribes.

The mirror was turned to destroy all those who didn't possess the mirror.

Chapter 67

I remember Jacko telling me his fears about the mirror. He was seated in the bell tower, his favorite place in the zoo. The old tower stood as a steeple on the large museum building that housed the gift shop and unseen administrative offices for the zookeepers. Within this bell tower, actually a daytime lookout for the headman of the zoo, Jacko sat cross-legged upon a leafy mat of willow branches. An old hermit, his mossy hair flying in orange wisps about his head, arms, and legs, Jacko looked out upon the park grounds with a great sadness in his eyes as he spoke.

"Newcomer, if there is a mirror in the zoo, then the deaths will start slowly. An animal will disappear here. Another turn up comatose there. Then nothing will happen for months. But the mirror is there, somewhere in hidden paws, the holder of the mirror learning to use it. That is one thing, the mirror is difficult to control.

And so, in secret the possessors of the mirror practice its use. Learn what must be done, how to hold it, how to focus its power. And eventually, they begin to use it more and more. More animals begin to fall into the sleeping death. More are lost. The zookeepers find more animals sleeping, but unwakeable in their cages. In fear of a new disease, the keepers get rid of these sleeping animals. They are taken to the secret trash pit in the back of the zoo and thrown down there. The unspeakable pit that no visitor has ever seen. And then the animals die there, unrescued, slipping into dreamless death."

I sat before Jacko unhappy, listening, with nothing to say.

Chapter 68

I felt a worry that I had not felt since gaining my astral freedom in the zoo.

Chapter 69

When Kory and I had first come to the zoo together, I had been worried. What I saw looked bad. Though there were elements of temple buildings on the zoo grounds, everywhere I saw animals in cages. Cages of all sizes, shapes, and constructions. Usually the size of the cage was just big enough to entice the animal to try to live there. Depending on the type of wild heart that lived within, the amount of roaming space the animal needed to survive, the zookeepers had designed the cage to provide just the smallest illusion of liberty.

But one look by Kory at all the animal faces and she was instantly frozen at the prospect of living in this zoo.

"Tip, all the animals, they look bored to death," whispered Kory.

Our cage was being ported in the back of a small zebra-striped golf cart.

"Yes, it looks like siesta time," I said.

"No," said Kory, "They look...so bored...something about them is dead. It's like they aren't really living in those cages," said Kory. I could hear the worry in her voice.

The zookeeper in blue uniform stopped the puttering cart. We were beside a large open structure. It was taller than the average tree, with wire about it, and dead tree trunks were leaning within it in a spider web of cargo ropes. Around this were other glassed in cages, and a few open paddies holding tall grasses and bushes. Behind all, a long brick hangar stood with a heavy metal door.

I didn't know it, but we had reached the primate house.

I didn't know it, but this was where I was destined to live the rest of my life.

Kory caught the scent of something.

"There are other monkeys here!" she cried. I could see this was an exciting prospect for Kory. After all, nearly all her life had been spent alone, separated from her kind, except for the few short months that she had now spent beside me.

At the prospect of being around other monkeys like ourselves, our spirits lifted a bit.

The blue uniformed zookeeper, his face always passive, he had nary an interest in us, took our cage off the zebra-striped golf cart and carried it through the metal door.

Thus, our corporeal bodies entered the primate house to stay.

Chapter 70

Because we were different monkeys, Kory and I were placed in separate cages and kept isolated for fifteen days. The room we were in was well-lighted, with white lacquer-painted walls, with blue smocked humans delivering food and inspecting us daily. It was something like the visits of the Algerian doctor, except there were no shelves of jarred animals and far less threatening.

We were given good foods, carrots, lettuce, and even bananas.

Kory and my hopes began to rise.

We'd had a few needles stuck in us, but neither Kory or I felt sick.

"I wish they hadn't put us in separate cages," I said.

"Why?" asked Kory innocently,

"I'd rather be anywhere, even in just another cage with you, than be in this one alone."

"Nice way to compliment a lady," said Kory with a sneer. Then she laughed.

I grimaced and muttered, "You know what I mean."

Chapter 71

But at the end of our quarantine, we became normal animals and our hopes were dashed. One morning the blue uniformed keepers came into the room and took Kory from her cage. I was not to see her again for nearly a year.

Later, I was taken out of my cage, carried in a box peppered with tiny airholes, and put into my new home.

It was this concrete box with fake hay, fake jungle vines, and a shiny aluminum tin of water to survive on.

And, of course, a big glass window with faces faces faces walking by.

Funny, but after several months in this cage, I could easily have the illusion that it was these faces in the cage, pacing by the glass, and I was looking in.

The monkey mind, it plays such bizarre tricks.

Beside my cage were the grey tribe of rockthrowers that were all to later die. To my right were some gibbons from Gibraltar, rock monkeys with very stuck up attitudes. As a newcomer, I looked at them through the glass and could see by the way they looked at me, taking no notice, not caring whether I was there or not, that they thought living on an island rock and taking food from tourists' hands was the best way of life any monkey could have. And they didn't care about anyone who didn't know it.

And then, I looked across the visitors hall at the cage facing mine. It had the same glassed in window and the same forlorn web of cargo rope, leafy jungle plants, turned over pots and pans, and a great orange orangutan sitting in a hump, like a keg, against the glass front of his cage. His face was actually mashed against the pane, his eyes, cheeks, and mouth flattened comically, as if someone had taken a rolling pin and smooshed them.

Above his cage was a sign in big red letters: Jacko.

I was to watch this orangutan sleep nearly continuously in his cage, except for brief spells of eating, drinking, defecating. I was to watch and watch him between his long bouts of sleep. And each time he looked my way, he raised a curved knobby finger in my direction. He pointed at me. Then drew his hands beneath his cheeks and closed his eyes.

I didn't know he was signaling me to sleep.

Chapter 72

Sitting in my glassed in cage, surrounded by the many other cages in the primate house, I felt a little monkey in a big place. I felt unimportant, a thing to be occasionally glanced at. Alone in the jungle, doing what I pleased, I had at least had the central importance of learning to throw rocks to defend my tribe. Here I felt little importance for anything I did. The zoo, the primate house would all continue around me whether I did anything at all. I felt adrift.

I wondered where Kory was. I wished she were with me. I would have liked to cling to her, see her reaction, just so that I knew I existed.

I grew used to the routine interruptions of the zookeepers. They came in nodding to me with unintelligible words, put down their tins of foods, and cleaned up the monkey poop in my cage a bit, not for me but to make the cage presentable for the visitors.

Day after day, I eventually learned to be indifferent to the faces.

I no longer saw the savage children growling, tapping, and even spitting on the glass. I no longer paid attention to the old wrinkle-faced women with feathered or veiled hats that looked on at me with either deep, but helpless concern or barely veiled distaste. I no longer took interest in the gorilla shaped males, fat men, who pulled their cheeks, shook their heads, and open-mouthed wagged their tongues at me. Making fun. Confident that they were free, they were standing on the right side of the glass.

What a ridiculous crowd.

What they were was impotent to help an animal struggling with its captivity, impotent to empathize or even understand, impotent to see us as wily animals with superb athletic abilities, born to range-free, born to survive in the toughest circumstances, the jungle. I expect what they saw was a monkey that was born to be in a cage.

They could ogle my brown face, my long furry tail, and believe I was in the cage I was supposed to be in.

So there was no help coming from that quarter.

Chapter 73

One of the characters in the primate house is Max. His full name, given him by some zookeeper on a lark, is Maxmillion Bananaman III. The sign over his cage simply reads: Max B. III.

Max knows how to draw a crowd.

At any one day in the primate house, five to ten people are grouped close before Max's cage, then suddenly jump back in startled fits of laughter. Max is one angry and crazy little chimpanzee and he is always putting on a show.

It is a show the zookeepers don't appreciate much.

I was later to learn that Max is one of the few animals that doesn't travel in his astral projection. He likes his little angry game so much, he refuses to dream.

Max is one to shake his head, wag his floppy ears, and screech making monkey faces at his on-lookers. Max is always bored and angry. His zookeepers always enter his cage carrying a stick.

But the visitors, they quickly get bored with angry pacing animals and move on. Max found no pleasure in screaming by himself. So he got more cunning.

He sits quietly in a huddle waiting for the next set of visitors.

When they stop, he jumps and gibbers to freeze them in their places.

Then, as they stand, he goes over and takes a handful of his feces and slings it at the window.

The crowd jumps back, surprised. Then they laugh.

This chimp has been clever enough to insult them. They recognize it. It's funny.

Max rolls on his back with laughter himself, his legs bicycle pedaling. He has a good time.

He puts on this performance once or twice an hour.

He attracts crowds.

And, of course, the zookeepers don't like this very much. They grumbling have to come in and wash his window everyday. They've tried to make Max stop, but there's nothing really they can do. What's the use in a zoo if you cover the glass or hide the animals from view where the visitors can't see them? So Max is always in his glassed-in cage behaving like that.

But it's its own punishment, Max's kind of behavior.

Once you sling shit on your window, you have to look out through it like that.

Chapter 74

In my first few months in the zoo, I had trouble sleeping. Strange dreams would erupt, grabbing my spirit, waking me with fear or awe. The kinds of dreams where you feel large animals poking their soft noses into your side to investigate you as you sleep. Then you realize a large animal is there, sniffing you, and you wake with a start. Sit up ready to screech, knowing the tiger is upon you.

Or the snake has wrapped round your neck and is tightening.

Or strange hawk faces are looking down on you with their fierce concern, staring some unintelligible message at you that makes you wake.

Once I was even startled from sleep by a large orangutan at my head, pulling my ear to get my attention. But when I woke, he wasn't there.

I sat up in the midnight blackness of my cage, drew my knees to my chest, and huddled in intense anxiety.

And there across the way sat Jacko, awake, staring at me with his glassy marble-black eyes.

I looked back at this animal staring at me out of the blackness of the monkey house.

He shook his head. He signaled me to sleep.

Chapter 75

In the cage to the left of Jacko is a mother howler. She has black black fur, and a long banana-ish nose. Her eyes are large. And with her long tail, long as a broom handle, she swings about her cage each day, all grace and motion. She moves in fast pendulum arches from branch to bar to rope, barely swinging for an instant on the object supporting her.

Her name is Tanya, and she's quite alone.

Howlers, especially mothers, like to be surrounded by other howlers and they tend to have many progeny.

Since Tanya was alone, she couldn't do that.

One day I noticed Tanya constantly looking up. In the top of her cage is a sky-light, one that opens a few inches to let in fresh air.

Tanya seemed to be constantly staring at it.

It wasn't for several minutes that I spotted what she was looking at.

A common sparrow was coming in the skylight and perching in the top branches of Tanya's leafy play structure. The sparrow was entering every few minutes with a thread of hay, a string, a feather, and depositing it in a clump in the branches.

Tanya sat in her cage looking up. She was fascinated.

The bird continued to zip in and out the skylight during the day, at times dropping its strand of hay or string to Tanya's cage floor.

Each time a strand hit the floor, Tanya leapt to pick it up.

She waited until the bird exited the skylight again.

Slowly Tanya would crawl up the climbing structure to the branch where the bird's clump of dry sticks and grass was hung.

She dragged herself to the top of her cage and carefully she took the fallen straw from her mouth and patted it onto the sparrow's pile.

Then she quickly dropped to the cage floor and waited for the sparrow to return.

Tanya was helping the bird build its nest.

Chapter 76

I watched Tanya and the bird over several weeks. I noticed that there was another sparrow that dared only enter the skylight for short periods. But the one sparrow grew more and more used to Tanya's cage, its smells, and its food. Each day Tanya would sit and watch the bird entering her cage. She gazed with such intensity, watching this living thing come to visit her.

Bit by bit, the bird perched on the leaf tops of her play structure, then moved to the lower branches, and finally, it felt at home hopping about the floor of the cage. Tanya, passive but interested, always watched this bird. The howler discovered the bird was most interested in the slices of dry bread that came in with Tanya's food. She learned to break and scatter crumbs for the bird to pursue and mop up on her floor.

Finally, the bird was as at ease in Tanya's cage as Tanya was. It flew in and out the skylight continually. It dropped and landed on the floor to prospect crumbs between Tanya's feet. It leapt and chirped freely in Tanya's leafy climbing tree. And Tanya, she wagged her head and mewed at it.

I watched as the bird would even land on Tanya's pate and sit looking boldly about the cage. Tanya only tilted her head and scratched herself in satisfaction.

Tanya had a pet.

And Tanya was happy.

So, good things do happen, even in a zoo.

Chapter 77

Over the months, having experienced the routine of the zoo, I grew more and more restless. Down from my skylight, open its plaintive inch to let in clean air, I could smell the fresh and flowery scent of Spring. Yet being in captivity, I didn't know how to get to it.

And in the distance, I could hear a high bobbling flute-like music. It seemed to ring continually in the primate house. I didn't know it yet, but it was the start of the summer season, and the music came from the turning of an ancient merry-go-round. Later, when I found out where this music emanated from, I was amazed to see this colorful old caravel, its bold statues of wooden animals, horses, rabbits, foxes, cats, all at run in an ancient endless circle, the animals in poses of running with all their hearts. Yet they were caught forever in an instant of action and the strain of life. It was an effect of great wonder to a monkey who had never experienced a view of human art before.

And in my cage that Spring, I felt that strain of restlessly moving, circling, and yet being motionless on a great wheel.

Chapter 78

Then one night I had a dream.

I had been restless and lonely all day. So that evening, I sat in the corner of my cage, my back to the wall, wondering what to do, when slowly I dozed off, dream images rising in my mind.

And then a monkey that I'd wanted to see was before me. It was Kory. She was standing, reaching for my hand, trying to pull me to my feet. She said nothing. I was in awe that she was here in my cage. In my dream, I could say nothing to her at all.

I let her pull me up. I felt elated. It was Kory, and I wanted so to see her. I moved silently behind her.

The scene changed to a long tunnel. Kory was walking quickly ahead of me down a winding cave. We were going deep underground. Every once in a while, Kory would stop, turning back to see that I was following. I tried to call out to her, express my happiness, but nothing would come out of my mouth.

I followed Kory deeper and deeper into this cave.

And finally, as we came to the end of it, I saw ahead a stone room holding a small wavering campfire. Lit on the walls of the cave were charcoal images of animals, a great tiger, its claws reaching out to catch, a great snake with the strength of an elephant, its mouth open to catch, and a bird mouth open singing atop a bush.

And there at the edge of the fire were two animals waiting for us.

I recognized the hairy old orangutan that lived in the cage across from mine. My eyebrows raised recognizing him. Still I could say nothing. The other animal was a leopard, fire shining in her eyes. I was later to learn her name was Linda.

Kory led me to the campfire, made me sit.

I sat, blinking, looking at the animals on the walls, looking at the faces of concern that I saw in Kory, the leopard, and this old orang who were facing me, without words.

I could not speak, I could not see beyond this cave. It was as if I were still alone, asleep, and could not come to consciousness to meet or have effect on these animals before me. I felt helpless.

The campfire was going dimmer. It was slowly burning out. Kory, the leopard, and the orangutan grew more concerned. Kory shook my shoulder, but I could only look at her.

The leopard approached me with its slow swaying grace. It stood before me, peering into my eyes. Then it said, "Young monkey, wake, you are in despair."

I was transfixed.

Then I found the head of the old orangutan near mine. He seemed to summon up great power from his bulky frame, then he leaned and put his mouth next to my ear.

And he said, "Unhappy monkey, wake in your dream, or die."

I heard this with my whole body.

And then I awoke. I was back in my cage, the light bright around me. I felt light, healthy, and strong. I felt the old animal. And as I looked about me, bewildered by the dream, I saw there in the corner, against the wall, was my body. Still asleep.

I was still a dream monkey.

Free in my cage.

As I realized this, I saw Kory step through the wall of my living quarters, come leaping across the cage floor, and pounce upon me in a giant tackling hug.

"I thought you would never wake!" laughed Kory as we wrestled.

I didn't understand a thing that had happened to me. But it was just fine.

Chapter 79

I was an astral being! A single sentence from Linda leopard had awaken me to my despair. A single sentence from Jacko had told me to wake or die.

And I had woken.

I looked around me in disbelief. An astral body, outside of my old self sleeping in the corner, what was I now? What did I believe in? I felt an utter freedom, simply because I was new. Obviously, the old laws didn't apply, look at my old self sleeping in the corner! I simply didn't belong to that container anymore.

I felt I could choose a new set of animal beliefs, those that would be good for me.

"Kory, I don't believe this!" I said. "Why didn't somebody tell me about this earlier? Why was I left alone in a cage?"

Kory sitting happily before me laughed, "You were asleep. We couldn't tell you. But you are awake now. Jacko and Linda saved you. As they came and saved me. Tip, wait till you hear, it's unbelievably wonderful. The cages mean nothing, you can step through them. You're free!"

"What?" I said, bewildered.

Kory rolled on her back, bicycling her legs, bowled over with glee.

I laughed at her, not entirely understanding. But something good seemed to have happened, had been shared with me.

Then the old orangutan stepped through the glass pane in the front of my cage. It was like an animal suddenly stepping out from behind a waterfall into view. He sat smiling at me a moment, then he spoke.

"Welcome to the astral zoo."

Chapter 80

Jacko spoke a few more words of encouragement to me, telling me that Kory had much to explain, so that for now, he would not stay.

"But before I go, remember newcomer, the zoo can be a place of joy and freedom, it will be according to your vision of it."

Jacko then lumbered out of sight through my back wall.

I looked at Kory, speechless.

Kory shrugged, smiling, "He's a wise old monk."

Chapter 81

Kory and I went for a walk outside my cage.

"Let me show you about the zoo," said Kory.

I looked back through the glass at my sleeping body in my old zoo enclosure.

Then I smiled. I was on the outside, looking in.

"Please do," I said. Then I grinned a monkey grin.

Kory chattered with laughter.

We monkey-loped down the primate house hallway to the steel door that had been closed to me now for months. Kory stopped and stood to the side.

I stopped and looked at her.

"Go through," she said, inclining her head toward the door.

I still wasn't used to passing through barriers. I shrugged and walked into the closed door, and passed right through.

I found myself outside, the zoo grounds bathed in hot August light.

Kory appeared through the door.

"It's night time. How come the zoo is lit up with sunlight like this?" I asked.

"For animals that must live in cages, locked up in their bodies during the day, that is the darkness of astral night. When animals leave those bodies and travel in their astral projections, that is astral day. The zoo fills with astral light and the fullness of the season. It's time to go out and play."

I looked around me at the greenery, the roaming animals, the Spring flowers. Then back at Kory.

For once it seemed good to be in a zoo.

Chapter 82

Kory took me for a tour around the zoo. Everywhere animals of all sizes and species were sitting, chewing, running, climbing among the park benches and fountains, sidewalks and buildings —all the animals minding their own business on their own. Here, laid out on picnic tables like dead drunks, slumped three sleeping gorillas. A slate gray elephant by the concession stand was tentatively putting his trunk into a garbage can and feeling around. Among the line of empty baby strollers, marmots were heedlessly scurrying and chasing each other in figure eights. A lion, his mane hirsute and fiery, was preening and calmly licking his paw in the toddlers' sand pit, ignoring a rhino only ten feet away rubbing his rump against an embarrassed-red fire hydrant. Ducks, swans, guinea fowl, and even ostriches were wandering across the park lawns occasionally stabbing their beaks at the ground.

"Isn't it fun?" said Kory as she led me past empty enclosures and sidewalks filled with animals.

"Whoa, what's that?" I said as a large hump appeared in the walkway ahead of us.

The hump grew and grew, then finally became a hippopotamus that pulled itself up out of the cement and went calmly to graze on a green lawn. I watched amazed.

"That is kind of surprising when they do that," laughed Kory. As I looked around at the suspect sidewalk all about me, Kory laughed, "you do feel they might come up under you at any time. But you get used to it. You know, hippos are grass mowers, they rarely bite."

I nodded uneasily.

"Come on, there's a lot to see," cried Kory. She seemed delighted to be leading the tour.

That astral day Kory spent leading me from place to place, the empty bear pits, the seal ponds now filled with sleeping gators, the llama and antelope barns which Kory cautiously pointed out were where the great boas and anacondas like to sleep in the rafters. It was bizarre to see the aviary with flights of colorful birds arrowing in and out through the walls like bees out of a hive.

"What's that over there?" I asked, pointing at a great mountainous slag heap of broken concrete washed and blackened by rain.

"We don't want to go there, that's where the baboons hang out," Kory grimaced, "Gross types. Come on, you've got to see the petting zoo!"

Kory ran off toward a large tree-filled area, lined with low fences, and various colorful climbing structures. I ran to catch up, running down sandy walkways bordered with hay bails and sitting stumps.

In the middle of the petting zoo stood a barn with a low sloping roof, and beside it yawned a wide duck pond holding shallow blue water. As if it were a beach, monkeys of all sizes were sunning on the barn roof, picking fleas, and prancing about. Every once in a while, a monkey would run with a great deal of prancing and chatter and fling itself off the roof to fall with a splash in the duck pond. Monkey after monkey was using the barn roof as a diving board. In the hot August sun, this running and diving looked like a lot of fun.

"Come on! Try it!" shouted Kory as she quickly climbed a drain spout on the barn wall. I leapt onto the spout and followed her up.

No sooner had Kory got to the roof than she chattered, ran, and jumped off into the air. I watched her splash into the calm water of the duck pond below. Several monkeys fell like bricks into the water around her as she surfaced and yelled at me to come on.

"Yeah," I cried, and I ran and jumped.

I splashed in over my head. It was something like the old days swinging over the Arkteepan creek.

I surfaced and monkey paddled to where Kory sat, drenched, at the pond edge.

"Isn't it fun?" said Kory, doing a quick dog-shake to get the water off.

"Yeah," I said.

"Let me show you where I like to live," said Kory. There was no stopping her, she was giving a whirl-wind tour.

I watched as she pranced off in an entirely new direction across the zoo.

It was all I could do to follow her bouncing tail.

After several minutes, we reached the shady grounds of a Eucalyptus grove. Kory picked out the tallest tree and began climbing toward the top. From where I sat at the tree's base, I could see these gargantuan trees, with they gracefully shaggy leaves and curved boughs, towering over the edge of the park.

I began to pick my way up to where Kory had disappeared into the heights above me.

I finally came to a fork in the high branches where a platform of sticks and soft bed of leaves were woven. Kory was sitting alone on this platform, looking out at the view from this high perch. There before her spread the whole zoo grounds, animated with animals, following their curiosities and seeking their pleasures. As I sat down beside her, I could hear calls, chatter, and laughter rising from all quarters of the zoo's bushes, fields, walkways, and structures. The high sky was blue, the smell of summer in the air.

Kory sat looking down on the zoo.

"It's beautiful," said Kory to me.

"Yes," I said.

"Rut with me now," said Kory.

And so I did.

And at the end of that astral day, I climbed higher into Kory's tall tree. I climbed to the top most branch, and then above all the zoo, I called:

"I am Tip, the rockthrower.

And joy exists!

It's true, oh all you zoo animals. Joy exists.

I know. I feel it."

Chapter 83

When traveling in your astral body, you must be careful. Although dream animals can't be killed, you can be caught. Even as a dream, it's unpleasant to be pounced upon by a tiger, shaken and eaten, digested, and excreted as tiger dung. Of course, the astral animal springs back to life, and a little water and bathing makes all good as new. Still it's an unpleasant experience. A nightmare really.

So the astral animals that wander the zoo behave much as they would in the jungle. The eaten keep a wary distance from the eaters. We know our astral projections are invulnerable, so there's a serenity that pervades the park grounds. But we do get in fights and squabbles. We do get pounced upon. For fun, practice, and even frustration. We're animals after all.

And we have the complete liberty of the park. No man-made object can hold us. You see, because we are living in our astral projections, no man-made barrier or construction can stop us. It has no meaning. We simply walk through the walls of our cages, monkeys slip easy as smoke through iron bars, snakes slide out through glass, the gators submerge in their concrete pools and surface in a sidewalk somewhere else in the zoo. Of course, trees, dirt, water, the real objects of Binah, our jungle mother, are real to us. We climb trees, we hide behind bushes, we graze in grasses just as in the liberty of our homelands. The things that were real to us as animals are real to our astral projections. It's just that, if you know how to do it, how to live in your astral projection, then no cage can hold you.

Man-made objects have no meaning other than what we attribute to them.

Chapter 84

"Kory?" I said.

"Yes?" said Kory, turning to me from munching an apple core that she'd found in the bushes. We were near the picnic area with its stout tortoise-like tables, grass, and flower beds.

"Do you like it here?" I asked.

"Yes," said Kory. "It's okay. Why do you ask?"

"I mean do you like it more than your home in the mountains? We've been here months and months, and it's all right here, I guess. But, do you ever think of leaving the zoo?"

Kory looked at me. We had been companions and lovers since leaving Africa, and now we had been close companions during our entire zoo life.

"I never knew my home. I was a just hopper when I was taken to my first cage. What's the use of thinking of that? We can't leave. Our bodies are sleeping in that place," said Kory. Her furry chin rose over her apple core to indicate the primate house, our primal prison. There had been mild distaste in her tone.

Jacko had explained how animals in their astral projections cannot leave the zoo. We animals could never travel farther away from our sleeping bodies than the last chain-link fence that marked the zoo's outer boundaries. An astral projection can never entirely leave its sponsoring body behind.

And so even the astral zoo had a captive population.

"It's just sometimes," I shrugged, "I think of my home. Arkteepa. It was, well, a place where I wanted to be. But here, I don't know. I enjoy it, of course."

"Because of me?" teased Kory.

"Of course," I said, "Above all because of you. Nothing I like better than going over and tearing up the tulip beds with you."

Kory laughed.

The week before we had gone on a happy monkey rampage and tore through the flowers around the wolf pens. We'd literally had a battle fighting with fistfuls of blue tulips, screeching with laughter, petals flying like butterflies blown to bits.

Kory and I had been breathless with laughter. A family of astral pigs had even come and sat in a line to watch our battle.

"I don't mind it here now," I said, "But do you ever think of escaping?"

"To where?" asked Kory.

That was the question I could never answer. It seemed we had no choice. We were stuck here with the zoo.

"Jacko, he said that some animals do escape. He has known of several. He says only the strongest and most cunning can do it."

"He also says your homeland is farther away than you can ever walk to, farther than a star," said Kory.

I didn't need to be reminded.

It was just that I was having trouble getting used to the idea that I was in this zoo to stay.

Indeed, I didn't really mind the zoo much. Knowing of my freedom to come with sleep, the dawning of astral day, I found I could tolerate the waking hours of my cage. It was just a needed respite from the full and thriving nightly activities in which we zoo animals participated within our dreams.

Kory and I chased obnoxious ground squirrels. We chattered fervently at the slinking wolves haunting the back bushes. We swung in complete loops and flips on the playground monkey bars, and we had even taken up the local monkey sport of hopping on the backs of indignant ostriches and riding rodeo-style, screeching with glee, until we were bucked off.

In the zoo, we had endless activities, as many as our imaginations could conjure.

One of my favorites was to sneak into the concession stand and take a single bite out of every doughnut leftover from the day. They would be served to the zookeepers with their coffee the next morning. It tickled me to think that I, a furry rockthrower, had taken the first bite.

And Kory, one of her favorite past-times was at the phone booth inside the front gate. She loved taking the phone off the hook and all night dialing wrong numbers. How many sleepers in the surrounding city had actually received a wakeup call from a monkey in the zoo? Thousands.

Kory said that she did it because she loved the squawks.

I also discovered even Jacko had his hobby. He collected postcards of animals from the gift shop. Comely primates mostly. The old codger had a little collection of beautiful hairy-legged maids that he liked to ogle, smacking his lips with satisfaction.

"You can't take the chimp out of the old ape," Jacko would laugh in self-depreciation.

Surprisingly, one of the mountain gorillas, Godzilla, had learned to drive the zebra-striped golf cart. Each morning the zookeepers would find it parked in a different place. They had heated arguments over who was doing it.

So mischief abounded at the zoo.

We astral animals found no limits for things to do.

Chapter 85

"Well, flea-picker, what are you doing here?"

I grimaced. I knew it was Randall and Buck, two long-haired red baboons who haunted the far reaches of the zoo. Although associated with the baboon pack, these two liked to wander about in their little cantankerous pair and make trouble.

I felt my ire rise as these age-old enemies of my tribe strode up with insufferable confidence.

I hated dealing with these two baboons.

I had been crossing the playground with a tomato that I'd saved from the cafeteria garbage can, heading for Kory's high lookout to share it with her.

I had just stopped to rest atop a small merry-go-round that kids push to turn. Randall and Buck were now prancing across the grassy fairway underneath the children's swings and across the sand pit, coming my way.

"What's that you got there, tick bait?" said Randall, hopping to a stop before the merry-go-round. Randall was a large, strong bull, and on all fours was about the size of a young goat. He was strong enough to snap a monkey leg with his bare hands, and he wanted everyone to know it. Buck, on the other hand, was a sullen-faced cur, with two narrowly spaced yellow eyes that drilled dislike at whatever was in front of him.

"Makes no difference what it is," said Buck, "He's going to give it to us."

I held the tomato between my paws, not moving or saying anything.

"So, turkey, let's have that tomato," laughed Randall.

"Randall," I said evenly, "I'm a rockthrower, not a turkey, you've got your animals mixed up again. Doesn't your fierce old leader, Elvis, teach you animal recognition?"

The most feared animal in the zoo was not the young tiger, Ramar, or even huge Beelzebub, the lion, an especially lazy male. It was Elvis, the leader of the baboon pack. He and fifty of his cohorts were known to descend on unsuspecting animals and tear them apart. And although the victim, his astral projection in pieces, came back to life the next day when his body woke, the scene of the pack's kill was painfully violent and horrific. Elvis and his pack of baboons were hated in the zoo.

"Recognize this, piss spot," said Buck. He snarled and opened his mouth wide, exposing the two white daggers of his canine fangs, each two inches long and needle-pointed.

Getting chomped by those would really hurt.

I tried to avoid these two asses whenever possible. But somehow, when confronted, I always felt my anger rise to meet them. And, of course, that's what they wanted. They had me out-weighed, out-muscled, and out-toothed, and so the worst confrontation would be a lark to them.

Finally, I could hold back no longer. "Listen, long-snouts, better go back and suck up to Elvis. What's that I smell? Baboons or horse shit?"

I gripped my tomato in one hand and stared at them, feeling the hair on the back of my neck raise like a dog's hackles.

"Hooo Hoooooo!" laughed Randall, "Buck, this monk wants a biting!"

"Well, if bite me must," grunted Buck smiling, his mean yellow eyes trained on me.

Randall loped to the other side of the merry-go-round in an attempt to get behind me. I turned so that I could watch both stalking baboons taking positions on each side.

I knew that at some unexpected moment they would both lunge together up onto the merry-go-round at me.

I was pissed now at being stalked by baboons. I decided it would be Randall.

Randall's eyes widened and both animals instantly tensed to leap.

But I leapt first. Straight up into the air four feet. And at the top of my leap, with the two baboons now charging over the merry-go-round at me, I threw.

The tomato exploded in blood-red shards in Randall's face.

Randall, blinded, missed and plunged under me, thumping into Buck, knocking the two in a screeching tangle that flopped on the merry-go-around platform.

I landed, jumped down from the merry-go-round and headed for the hedge that protected the playground. I ran like hell.

I didn't want these two chumps to catch me.

Once safe in the hedge where I knew they could never run me down, I called back at the screeching baboons, Randall, still blind, madly attacking Buck.

"Long snouts, you guys deserve each other! Why don't you get together and start a family? Baboon-style," I called.

I realized it was a loutish thing to say, but I was feeling very baboonish myself.

Chapter 86

More and more the mirror made its presence known. A marmot here, mysteriously asleep, a koala there, hanging by one foot in his tree, unwakeable.

Animals die all the time in the zoo, of course. The old wear out, go blind, lose strength, and fail. The despondent give up. The misunderstood and ill-housed get sick from their unmet needs. The tamest animals go berserk, explode with frustration, hurt a human, and have to be put down. The zookeepers get out the death carts.

They haul the animal garbage away.

The zookeepers have rules about disposing of animal bodies. They can't just toss a stiff carcass of an exotic animal over the zoo fence and forget about it. They'd hate to have a human third-grader show up at school sporting a necklace of still bloody tiger claws.

And they certainly can't throw the corpse of one animal into the next cage for another animal to eat. They don't want to spread disease.

The animal doctor who tends to the zoo, he doesn't always want to find out the source of death, the illness that kills. He wants to tend the sick and make them well. Once Keth, the elephant god, has carried away an animal spirit on his back, then for a vet, it's too late, and not much use looking under the animal's skin to see the source of destruction.

Besides, when an animal dies from lack of caring, there's usually not much to see.

The other animals isolated in their cages aren't much exposed to intruding sickness. So most of the dead are disposed of without going far into why they died. An animal catches the flu, another animal succumb to tuberculosis. The zookeepers don't ask why it caught the flu when animals in the wild don't die of flu, why this animal became susceptible to tuberculosis when healthy lungs roar all over the jungle. It's a premise of the zoo conditions that certain animals get sick and die.

When there are troubling deaths, however, the zookeepers take a different tact. When there are deaths that seem to spread across the zoo, first they don't worry about it. It may take a certain kind of animal out, those effeminate gazelles, those bullish, rutting capybara, the weak or less suitable for zoo life. But that's not a worry. The zookeepers never worry about replacing any one kind of animal species. But when the sickness begins to move from cage to cage, is unknown, and they have no cure, the zookeepers become worried. They worry about all the animals dying. They worry about having a zoo that is a disaster. They worry about how they will look when there's an epidemic in a zoo under their care. They worry a mite about catching the disease themselves.

And, of course, to be fair, there are an ardent few keepers who worry tremendously that their favorite animal might die.

So they seek to protect us.

They also seek to protect all the living beings outside the zoo.

They don't go into the cage of the dead and tag and bag them, hump them onto a zebra-striped golf cart and haul them to the bin that goes to the dump. You can't just take them to the dump where God knows what animal will feed on them. Spread disease.

The zoo has a secret garbage pit for the contaminated and contagious. The unconscious sleeping marmot, the dead-asleep koala are taken by gloved hands and tossed into the pit. There they sleep to death or until the pit is covered over with dirt a week or two later and these animals are forever buried.

Out of sight and out of mind.

That's the zookeepers' rule for the visitors.

Chapter 87

One Saturday morning in the primate house, an especially crowded day of endlessly passing families, parent's leading children and pushing strollers, I was sitting in my cage looking out its window. I noticed that the visitors were consistently walking past Max the mad chimp's cage without stopping.

Strange.

I hopped over to the very edge of my cage window to squeeze a look into Max's display.

There he was asleep, laying across his overturned water tub, his head and face down on the floor.

He looked dead.

The visitors would look in and then step back a step, then quickly move on. They were unsure whether this animal was ill, dead, or sleeping, and so uneasy they hastened on. Especially those that knew of Max's trick. They knew that sleeping on the job was not like Max.

The downed chimp didn't move a muscle all day.

I watched with growing concern.

And then near six o'clock, an hour after the zoo closed, a zookeeper entered Max's cage and poked him in the side with a stick.

Max didn't move.

The zookeeper hauled his limp body from the cage.

Chapter 88

"It makes sense," said Jacko gravely rubbing his chin, "He was an easy target."

"But he didn't travel in his astral projection. How did they get to him?" I asked.

"If it is the baboons, then they went to him. They knew he wouldn't be leaving his cage. They knew of his angry chimpy-ness and knew he was penned in. He would be alone here in the primate house while we were all out in the zoo. I think they went to him and simply entered his dream with the mirror. Max would be a quick victim once he saw it."

"Why are they doing this? It's horrible. It's ghastly. Why kill zoo animals. We don't hurt anything," cried Kory outraged that something was so deeply wrong in her house.

"I can only guess," sighed Jacko, "But the sense of it to me is that if there are only baboons in the zoo, then there is more zoo for the baboons. Less to share. More to have. So they are clearing the zoo of animals unlike them. They insist, are willing to kill so that this place might be a zoo solely of baboons."

"Impossible," I said. "They can't kill us all. Besides, the zookeepers would just keep bringing animals in."

Jacko shook his head. "They would bring fewer until they were sure the disease had stopped. And the disease wouldn't stop until all the remaining animals cowered before the baboons and submitted to whatever they wanted, submitted to their baboon vision of zoo life. Then there would be no need to kill more animals with the mirror."

Then Jacko looked at both Kory and I sitting uneasily in his bell tower.

"And, of course, by then, most of the animals like you would be dead."

"So we have to kill them all," muttered Kory, seething with anger.

"No, Kory," cautioned Jacko, "You must watch out for that. You can become a victim of the mirror yourself if you don't."

"Why? How does it work? How does the mirror paralyze the astral animals?" I asked.

"I know only the old stories told me by the orang before me. He told me that the secret of the mirror is that it works perfectly."

"What does that mean?" I asked puzzled.

Jacko shrugged, unsure. "The holder of the mirror does not show it to his victim right away. The baboons select a victim and in number go out to meet it. They surround the animal and intimidate it. They threaten and squawk. They taunt and call names, they seek to raise the ire of this animal, so that it will want to act against them. That's why Max would be an easy target. They shriek and show their baboon fangs as they insult. "

"And, eventually, the unknowing animal reflects their anger back. The animal growls, raises its anger, and bares its fangs to fight, expecting to be pounced upon and torn to pieces."

"And then they show the animal the mirror."

Jacko stopped to consider his words.

"And the animal looks deeply into the mirror and is frozen by what it sees. It sees only its self. It is surrounded by fierce baboons, and in the mirror it sees only its own anger. It sees it is not a fierce baboon pack. It looks into the mirror and sees a single astral animal, angry and outnumbered, reflected perfectly back at itself. And it is like two mirrors facing each other. The image of the astral being stretches into infinity. The astral animal becomes lost, paralyzed."

"So what do we do?" asked Kory.

"The animal cannot wake up until it is released from the mirror. The mirror must be broken so that the animal can become itself again."

"How do we do that?" I asked.

"I don't know," grunted Jacko unhappily. "Of course, the baboons hide the mirror. And of course, they only show it to you when they mean to use it. The last old orang, he told me there had once been a mirror, long ago, and it had been destroyed. But he didn't know exactly how. He only knew what the animal did before breaking it."

"Who destroyed it?" I asked.

Jack shrugged, "He said it was a white monkey."

Chapter 89

Each astral day as Kory and I went out to forage, we bumped into frightened animals, tense and wary. We would come around a grassy corner of an animal house to find a coven of rabbits, ears up and alert, spot us then burst in a flurry of hopping under the hedges. We sat on park bench to see Beelzebub, the lion male, get up from the kid's sand pit and jog away. He'd heard a rustling in the bushes that drew his suspicions, although it turned out to be only a guinea hen and rooster fighting to mate. The ostriches were constantly turning their head in nearly complete circles as they walked. The whole zoo was nervous and watchful.

From my roost on the park bench, I could see the suspected source of all this uneasiness. There at the far side of the zoo stood a great mountain of broken concrete and gravel and boulders. It was surrounded by a deep concrete moat. Scraggly bushes without leaves stood out here and there on the slag heap like brooms stuck into the ground by their handles. Although there were no animals in sight, this rough living space was the heap where the baboon pack was kept. Behind the keep were many caves and caverns made of piled slabs and rocks. This was where a modest gathering of five baboons had once been housed in the zoo.

But with time, according to Jacko, the baboons had multiplied until there were thirty or forty, in vastly overcrowded conditions for simians. The zookeepers hadn't noticed, but subtly the organization of the baboon populace had changed. It had become more violent. More harsh. The young were sometimes bitten badly when they intruded into an adult's sleeping range. Food was not shared well. Dominance became more important. And finally, a leader like Elvis arrived. And essentially he ruled using bloody tooth and claw.

Elvis' ascension to leader had been marked by the zookeepers finding the body of an elder baboon chewed to pieces in the moat. And that day, Elvis had walked the heap a king among his tribe, even though his tail was bloody and shorter.

The place also smelled to high heaven. It reeked of baboon scents and piss. My back shivered and my stomach rose just looking at it even from here, at a great distance.

Now the zoo animals avoided going near the heap at any cost. First, they didn't think anything worth exploring would be in the baboons keep. Second, they didn't want to attract the violence of the pack by going there.

A single baboon sentry was always posted at the top of the slag head day and night. With a single call, the pack would appear running over the crest of the heap. And once they came running, they ran after any animal that they might catch.

You had only to see one animal caught, torn limb from limb, by laughing and bloodthirsty baboons, to know it was a good idea to stay as far back from the baboon keep as you could.

Chapter 90

Kory and I were searching through the low scrub at the back of the zoo for chickens eggs, when I heard a terrific rustling on a low knoll a few yards away. I put my hand on Kory's shoulder to make her be still.

Two alerted primates, we both peered through the tall grass at the knoll. The rustling continued like the struggling of a boa with a four-legged creature. Kory and I froze watching in secret.

Just then four baboons appeared walking about the base of the knoll. They were dragging something, and it was struggling not to be dragged.

It was a small kangaroo whelp, silently and frantically hopping to pull away. Three baboons had it firmly by the tail, pulling it like fireman pulling a hose, with another at the kangaroo's chest, pulling on the animal's pouch.

Just then, a great lion-like baboon, with wide muddy mane, jumped to the knoll top in a single bound. It sat, its large muzzle cocked in a fierce sneer, looking down on the struggle below. The large baboon's shoulders were marked by scars from monkey battles, its reddish chest and haunches strong, its boney tail standing up straight but bitten short by three inches.

"Lay that kicker down, so I can get to it," commanded the baboon.

I looked quietly toward Kory and whispered, "It's Elvis."

Kory's eyes widened.

As we looked on at the leader of the baboons, I suspected we were watching some baboon experiment. I felt my ire raise, telling me I was a rockthrower after all.

The four baboons pulling the kangaroo now pounced upon it and held it down. The exhausted animal was still struggling, whipping its tail and kicking sporadically.

"Can I bite it to make it be quiet?" called one of the baboons up to their leader. I recognized the ugly mug of the yellow-eyed Buck.

"Certainly!" called Elvis, "Get that animal still! But leave his eyes free, he has to be able to see!"

At that Buck bent and gave a tremendous bite to the Kangaroo's haunch. The kicking animal mewed in pain. The other baboons squatted upon it, holding its limbs down as they sat upon its shoulder, body, and head.

"What are they doing? What are those thugs doing?" asked Kory in alarm.

"Their being baboons," I said with disgust.

Elvis had now stood up and was searching the perimeter of the grassy knoll with his eyes. Satisfied that no other animal was in view, he signaled behind him.

I watched as a smaller baboon trotted up the slope carrying something at his chest.

"I'm not standing for this!" cried Kory, "If they're looking for secrecy, they haven't got it."

Kory jumped up and scrambled through the dry grasses toward the knoll. The commotion of her movements alerted the baboon group and they turned their gaze toward her.

"Who's there?" roared Elvis. He was suddenly alert, standing on hind legs looking at Kory. He hastily signaled to the approaching monk behind to retreat, and this short baboon, still holding something to his chest, stopped, then turned tail and ran from sight behind the knoll.

"I see what you're doing, you big bags of dung! Picking on the silent ones! Let that kangaroo go! You baboon monsters!"

Kory was approaching fearlessly.

The four baboons sitting on the kangaroo hesitated and looked up at their boss to see what to do.

"Do we kill her?" asked Buck with some eagerness. "I can catch that little whiptail monk and bite her legs off."

"Not on your life, you yellow-tongued drinker of hyena piss," cried Kory. I was amazed at how riled up she was. Confronting a pack of baboons was dangerous play.

Instinctively, I looked around and gathered several large rocks.

"Well, rather than make this a long chase, wait one second," said Elvis. Elvis raised a commanding paw.

Then a wide rustling started up in the grasses all around. I could see many baboon heads, thirty or forty, leaping toward the knoll. Elvis had summoned the whole pack.

"When I signal, we all catch her," cried Elvis, "Then we'll have two animals to play with as we like. But no killing until they've seen our little play thing!"

Kory was now looking around at the baboons running through the grasses to encircle her. Instead of fleeing, as I expected her to, Kory charged to the attack.

She scampered directly to the four holding the kangaroo and nipped Buck hard on the end of his tail. Buck screeched and leapt straight into the air. Kory, angry as a bulldog, charged the remaining three with such ferocity, they fell back aghast.

The kangaroo stood up, wobbling for a moment.

"You faint-hearted prairie dogs. Get her!" screamed Elvis. "She can't nip you deep! Tear off her tail!"

Then I saw a baboon charging Kory from behind.

"Kory, run!" I shouted.

Kory cringed, then ran in my direction. I jumped up and threw the rocks with all my might. One of the rocks luckily hit the side of Kory's pursuer with a drum-like thump, slowing him to a three-legged pursuit, and Kory quickly out-distanced him.

The kangaroo, dazed and bewildered, was scuttling away unnoticed. The baboon packs' attention was focused on Kory sprinting my way.

I found another rock and tossed it high. Elvis was forced to duck from the top of the knoll.

"Get those scabby tails," shouted Elvis. "Nobody attacks Elvis, and nobody flaunts the pack."

Kory reached me, and I turned, and we ran together toward the low hedge. I knew once we were in it, no baboon could catch us as we leapt from low to high branches. I could see now we would easily make the eucalyptus trees where the baboons couldn't follow us into the heights.

Kory was panting and running beside me with all her might.

"Baboon filth, I hate them!" she gasped as she ran.

I looked over at her surprised. Her anger, even during hot pursuit, was supreme.

Chapter 91

"What were they doing with that kangaroo?" said Kory.

We were both seated, resting in Kory's high nest, safe in the eucalyptus tops.

"Kory that was dangerous, you can't just charge a pack of baboons like that," I complained.

"Why not?" asked Kory. She really didn't know. It was as if she had such confidence in her abilities and anger that she felt invulnerable. She would charge anything she didn't like at any cost.

I shook my head. Kory had seen something she didn't like and she had to react in a very specific way to it. She had seen an outrage and so had reflected her outrage back.

"You know that short baboon?" I said, "I think he was carrying the mirror. I think they were going to use it on that kangaroo."

Kory frowned. I frowned as well realizing the mirror had been so close to us. If we had been caught, it might have meant our end right there.

"Kory that was dangerous," I said.

"That Elvis, he sure is a creep. Someone ought to bite off his tail," said Kory.

I didn't remind Kory that someone had already partially done so.

"We came close to the mirror," I said

Kory nodded. She was silent for a brief moment.

"Do you think we could break it?" she asked.

"I don't know, Kory. We don't know anything about it. I'm sure the baboons keep it hidden and guarded. I doubt we could ever get through the pack to steal the mirror."

Kory looked at me.

She said nothing.

But her monkey jaws were firmly clenched.

A bad sign in a little Berber monkey.

Chapter 92

"So it *is* the baboons who hold the mirror," nodded Jacko gravely.

We had just finished telling him of the assault on the kangaroo, our flight from Elvis and the pack, and the short baboon who had carried off an unseen object.

Kory had reported her involvement with charging the pack with a fiery enthusiasm. Such that Jacko had raised his hairy arm, taken his chin in his fingers, and looked at her with growing concern in his small black eyes.

"We must do something now," said Kory, "They're going around getting rid of the silent ones and the helpless. The small ones are next, then all."

Jacko nodded. He pursed his lips as a sign confirming the utter truth of this.

"What can we do?" I asked.

"We'll go there," said Jacko.

"Where?" I said.

Kory, looking at Jacko, had already comprehended. She turned to me and said, "To the heap."

"We're going the baboon mountain? That's the fastest way to get torn apart."

"We'll go there," said Jacko. "I'll get a few of the other apes. Godzilla the gorilla clan-master, he'll come. Hooter and Scooter, the squirrel monkeys and vine-flyers, they will help us. They are natural spies."

"When do we go?" asked Kory.

Jacko looked at Kory.

"Tonight."

Chapter 93

The smell was already getting bad. The baboon heap was just fifty yards ahead, and our little group of primate insurgents were low-slinking through the last hedge.

Oddly, it was the smallest of our band, Hooter and Scooter, the vine-flyers, who were making the most noise, rustling the dry leaves as they walked. Godzilla, the huge old gorilla, was picking his way through the brush in near silence, his natural way.

"The sentry is there," said Kory, pointing to the top of the heap.

Jacko pushed aside two leafy branches for a better view. He nodded. Then he pointed silently toward the side of the baboon keep, where a low building holding lawn mowers and other zoo gardening equipment stretched along the backside of the keep.

"We'll go in there," said Jacko. "On the other end of that building is a thicket. We'll watch from the thicket."

"What do we do if they see us?" I asked.

"We kick tails," grunted Godzilla. He drew back his lips in a toothy gorilla smile.

"No, we're here to find out where the mirror is," interrupted Jacko. "We retreat, until we have a plan."

"Unless we can get it and break it right there," I said.

"Okay, let's go," said Jacko. Jacko pointed for Hooter and Scooter the smallest to go first to check out the way. Then Kory hopped in line, followed by me, Jacko, and Godzilla.

We crept Indian-file down the outer edge of the heap. I was breathing through my open mouth to avoid the down-wind stench.

We finally reached the concrete wall of the garden tool shop. I could hear baboon grunts and an occasionally screech come from inside the heap, but Jacko shook his head that none of us should look above the low wall into the heap.

Hooter and Scooter leapt through the shop wall and disappeared. Kory then went through the wall into the shop.

I followed her in, waiting for my eyes to adjust to the dimness of the shed interior, filled with dank smells of cut and rotting grasses, before moving among the silent and angular mowers and stationery garden tools. I could just see Kory's shadowy outline moving at the far end of the shop. I hopped forward to be nearer to her.

Jacko came through the wall and bumped into a rake, which he caught with a grab from his long arm before the tool clattered to the floor. I saw his shoulder's lower as he breathed a sigh of relief. Kory had just disappeared through the far shop wall when the great head and then body of Godzilla strode into the shop.

Even in the darkness, he walked with complete confidence through the shop, touching nothing as he passed among the many dimly seen obstacles. It struck me with wonder how a five hundred pound gorilla could walk noiselessly through a darkened garden shed.

We all exited the shop wall and regrouped under a low arch of wiry leaves and branches.

"Okay, let's take a look. But don't let them see you. Hooter and Scooter, check it out first."

The two small squirrel monkeys, hairy-faced with big eyes like small-headed owls, both nodded. They turned and climbed silently up several branches until they could see down across the concrete moat into the baboon heap.

"What do you see?" I whispered up to them.

"Some kind of a meeting. It looks like the pack is gathering."

Jacko nodded. He hunched his shoulder toward the heap, we all crept silently forward to take a look.

Chapter 94

"Gather in! Gather in! All boons, you are commanded to attend!" a large bullish baboon was shouting down from mid-heap to the milling pack below. I recognized Randall calling in the tribe.

An unorganized crowd of baboons of all sizes was wandering about the floor of the heap. More were now appearing, hopping out the black cavernous windows that dotted the back side of the heap. A steady train of baboons, their reddish fur shining and long tails curled, were loping toward Randall. I scanned the sides of the heap but didn't see Elvis anywhere.

At the very top of the heap, a small baboon, nearly an imp, was squatting. His head turned constantly like a search light as he looked all about. Randall looked up at this short sentry, hooted, and the sentry nodded that the coast was clear.

Randall signaled with a hand wave toward a black cavern behind him.

The baboon pack, now gathered at the base of the heap, moved expectantly, looking up at Randall and the black den opening.

Then Elvis appeared. He walked out of the dark den with a swaggering slowness that was meant to imitate majesty.

"Welcome boons, kats, kits, and whippets! I am glad to see you all!" called Elvis over the heads of the pack, "I behold you in your strength and baboon beauty. Pack up!"

"Pack up!" shouted all the baboons eagerly in return.

"Pack up!" shouted Elvis again.

"Pack up, Pack up, Pack up!" crowed the baboon crowd enthusiastically from below. The many baboons, even the young, were pushing and shoving each other rowdily, as their leader sat and looked out over them with satisfaction.

"Elvis! Elvis! Elvis!" chanted a small contingent on the outside of the pack.

I heard a low growl next to me. Surprised, I looked over to see Godzilla crouching beside the wall, his face scrunched in a snarl. A leader of his own clan, he didn't like what he saw. Jacko bobbed his head and put his finger to his lips for silence. Godzilla stopped his growling.

Jacko looked over at me with a raised eyebrow to signal his nervousness that the huge old gorilla might do something to give our hiding place away. I looked back at Godzilla, now resting silent and gazing on the heap, hoping, too, he wouldn't do anything to call the pack down on us.

I didn't see any stones around at all, except a lot of loose gravel at the bottom of the heap floor.

Kory, crouched behind the wall next to me, was frowning deeply.

"Gentle baboon folk," started Elvis over the shrieking clamor of the crowd below. He raised his paws beside his ears and the baboons slowly fell silent.

"As you know, we baboons have the power, a new power, to transform this place, this zoo, into a paradise."

The baboon tails were now lowering as the crowd sat. Many baboons were nodding as they listened up toward their leader.

"Soon, we will control the zoo. We, you and I, the pack that supports and loves you, will hold this zoo in our paws!"

Elvis put out his two paws as if to catch a fruit tossed to him.

This statement was met with much excited hooting and tail whipping.

"But I want you all, before we take our new weapon on the hunt, I want you all to know why we possess this power, why we are the baboons to rule this roost."

"Elvis, Elvis, Elvis." The low chant started again somewhere within the pack. Elvis raised his paws for quiet.

"If we all know why we are what we are, if we all understand the secret of the pack, then we are invincible!"

"Right on, your high furriness!" shouted a baboon voice. It was the yellow-eyed Buck, calling from below with both paws to his mouth.

"This reek is too much," whispered Kory next to me, "I'm going to throw up." I thought Kory was being sarcastic until I saw her hunch over.

I patted Kory on the back as she bent gagging.

"Kory, you sure you want to stay here?" I asked.

Blinking through tears of distaste, Kory nodded yes.

I turned back to look at Elvis speaking to his tribe.

"WE have the weapon! We have the power! WE are the ones to wield it, we have learned to use it wisely!" shouted Elvis. His stubby baboon tail was up, and he stretched a long arm back, pointing into the darkness of his lair.

"It's there!" said Jacko, "He must keep it in there where he sleeps!"

I nodded. It was likely the mirror was hidden in the depths of Elvis' black den. But I didn't see much chance of getting past the sentries, this surrounding pack, and into the den to look for it.

"But the weapon is not the power!" cautioned Elvis.

"The pack, the power is the pack, pack up!" shouted a know-it-all baboon from the center of the crowd.

Elvis looked down at this caller with a sneer.

"No, idiot. It is not even the pack which holds the power."

The baboons, whose credo was power to the pack, were suddenly mystified. I could see them scratching heads and thighs contemplatively, trying to fathom Elvis' nulling of their birthright: faith in the pack.

"The power comes from a much more subtler source. When we band together, then we know the power of the pack. The power that lets us take any tail for a trophy, that let's us gain our collective will. But the source of that power we must be clear about!"

"The mirror! The source of power is the mirror!" shouted another from the crowd.

Elvis sat back and laughed, as if at a misunderstanding children.

"Our power, the power to rule this zoo is not even the mirror! Boons, hear me! We have the mirror because first we have the power! The mirror is our tool! It came to us. With it we will create the new soul of the zoo, and we will freeze the soul of anyone who stands in the way. You, brave hearts, have seen our success."

"Yes, yes!" shouted a baboon.

Just then Kory bent beside me and threw up miserably.

I looked down on her, but there was nothing I could do.

I looked up to check Hooter and Scooter's position in the branches overhead. They were bending far out over the branches to hear Elvis' words. They each had puzzled and worried looks on their owlish faces.

Elvis signaled behind him. Then a short baboon leaped out of the darkness and held a shining object high over his head. There was as brief diamond flash of astral light.

The baboon crowd roared with approval.

"The mirror!" said Jacko, catching his breath.

"That is it! Our weapon! No animal can resist it, resist us, when we turn it upon him. We alone, the boon pack, have conquered and learned the use of the mirror. No other pack in the zoo shall have or use it! But why? You must understand that. Why do we baboons have this power? Why is it that we can bite the tail from any victim we choose?"

"If only there was a rock, I might be able to hit it from here," I whispered to Jacko. Godzilla looked over at me and nodded. We all looked around, but indeed there were no rocks near.

"But it's so close!" frowned Godzilla looking back at the ranting baboon pack. Godzilla let go a low growl of exasperation.

Elvis was now standing, calling to quiet the hooting pack.

"Our source of power is not the mirror, my tribe," said Elvis calmly. "If you know this secret, then you will know our wealth. Our power, our true power, is in each baboon heart that beats before me. It is in you! And in a very simple way. Each of you baboons knows this, though perhaps you never speak it. Each individual baboon among us is a superior animal in this zoo. You are superior in your baboon beauty, superior in your thoughts, you are superior in your speed, and superior in love and anger and viciousness! And you are lonely!"

The calls of the many rose toward Elvis' up-stretched arms.

"Oh my tribe, each with your superiority, you are a lonely animal. Those other animals, unlike you, how can you share with them the beauty of being a baboon, the grandeur of your leaps, the incredible untiring strength of your legs? You cannot share with them, they cannot understand the powers of mind, paw, and fang that are yours. You cannot share with them the incredible wonder of being a baboon! And so these other animals, of lesser gifts, they have little to interest you. You, in the jungle, with the gifts of Binah, our jungle mother, the power of Keth, carrier of the sun, you dear pack-mate ARE ALONE!"

"You dear pack-mate are alone, the animal at the top of the tree of evolution. And your loneliness is great!"

"Yes! Yes!" shouted voices from the crowd.

"And so, you naturally seek to be among those that share your powers. Naturally, you look to surround yourself with those most like you. Naturally the superior flock together. Those that know the superiority of your heart, that know the superiority of your interests, and the superiority of your beast! You slake your loneliness, your superior needs among those who can understand and support you! You band together with like hearts, seeking a better world with other like hearts."

"And that is the source of our second great power!" shouted Elvis. He jumped high, waving his arms wildly over the crowd. "That is the source of our second great power: the pack!"

The baboon pack erupted in jubilant howls and hooting.

"Pack up! Pack up! Pack up!" the crowd began chanting.

"And from that, comes our third great power!" shouted Elvis over the bugling crowd, "The mirror! We can use the mirror to show the truth! We use the mirror to show the other animals who they are! We use the mirror to spread the vision of the pack! And when we show those jungle animals...wait...those zoo animals the mirror. Then they see the truth, they see us, the baboon pack, and they see themselves, and they cannot stand before it. They are lost."

"So tails up, baboons, for this zoo will be ours!" screamed Elvis with an amazing trembling fury.

All the baboon pack was now rolling and kicking with glee on the ground before him.

"So he thinks loneliness and superiority are the source of his power," muttered Jacko next to me, his mouth rippling as he looked out on this spectacle.

"So we'll make this zoo better for all of us, better for the baboon, and even for lesser animals!" cried Elvis.

"We'd best go," said Jacko, "We must plan."

Chapter 95

It was just then that there was a crack overhead. I looked up to see Hooter and Scooter dangling from a long limb broken three or four feet above them. Then the branch let go, and the two clinging monkeys toppled into the baboon moat. They hit the concrete some ten feet down with a sickening thump that I feared spelled injury.

I leapt to the top of the wall and looked down on Hooter and Scooter lying below.

The entire baboon pack had turned to look behind at the noise. Then they spotted the two monkeys on the moat floor, struggling to get untangled from the branch fallen on them.

Kory was beside me, then Jacko, leaning on the wall top, stretching our arms out toward Hooter and Scooter.

"Jump! Jump up to us!" yelled Jacko down at the dazed squirrel monkeys.

"Kill them! Intruders! Kill them" shouted Elvis, pointing at us. "They've seen the mirror! Kill them! Pack up!"

At that the baboon pack rose and began bounding toward us in a flooding wave.

Hooter and Scooter, still unsteady from their fall, were wobbling toward the base of the wall and our dangling arms.

Hooter made a weak jump, but fell three feet short of Jacko's outstretched paw.

"Get a stick to lower to them!" shouted Kory at me. I could see the pack racing toward them, now only several leaps away. The baboon faces were all raging eyes and bared fangs.

I saw no hope of finding a stick and lowering it on time.

"We can't save them, we must flee!" shouted Jacko.

Then there was a great roar behind us.

I turned to see Godzilla standing his full height, arms waving over his head, bellowing with a full chest.

Then he leapt over the wall and down into the baboon pit.

He hit the concrete beside Hooter and Scooter, roared again, and then charged the pack. The enraged five-hundred pound gorilla charged headlong into the on-coming baboons. The first baboons were skidding to a halt.

Godzilla ran into the pack, grabbing up baboons and swinging and tossing them out of his way with incredible might and ferocity. The baboons, frightened, were temporarily falling back.

I jumped down over the wall and followed Godzilla into the pit. He was wading into the pack, breaking arms, biting hips, and shaking and tossing his victims left and right.

"Pack up!" shouted Elvis, seeing this black mountain gorilla working his way through the baboon crowd toward him.

Once on the concrete floor, I ran to the broken branch, and began dragging it over the side of the moat. It was just long enough that I hoped Hooter and Scooter could climb it like a ladder and leap to Jacko's outstretched arms.

Then something plopped down beside me. It was Kory. She began helping me drag the branch to the side of the moat as well.

"Pack up and kill them all!" shouted Elvis.

The baboons had fallen back from Godzilla who was roaring and bounding in all directions after them. As the group scattered, he could no longer catch them as they scampered from reach.

The branch was up, Kory and I holding its base. Hooter and Scooter were quick to climb the slanting limb and one by one leapt up to Jacko's dangling hand, and were pulled to safety.

I looked back at the pack. Godzilla had now turned and was looking up at the screeching Elvis.

"Pack up! Kill that ape before he gets the mirror!" At that Elvis signaled the baboon holding the mirror to retreat into the nearby cavern.

Godzilla roared and renewed his charge up toward Elvis.

But by this time, the pack had reformed, and in a encircling onslaught of bodies, dozens of baboons leapt upon the gorilla. Soon Godzilla had three and four baboons on each arm and leg, biting and slashing with their teeth. More baboons were clawing in a heap up the struggling gorilla's back. I could see that even Godzilla would be no match for the entire pack once they fell upon him.

"Go up!" I shouted at Kory. But she shook her head.

"You need the branch, climb it!" she yelled, "I can leap it from here."

I suddenly understood that I was in the same predicament as Hooter and Scooter, the wall was too high for me to jump.

I turned and climbed the limb as Kory held it.

The roars of Godzilla, fighting, covered now in biting baboon savagery, were echoing behind me.

I leapt and Jacko's hand caught mine and the orang jerked me up to safety.

Hooter and Scooter were squatting on the wall, screeching encouragement to Kory.

Then Kory leapt. It a single magnificent bound, she was up there among us. I sensed Jacko was badly shaken. I could see the old orang was panting and trembling with the frantic activity.

We all looked back out at Godzilla fighting the pack.

We could see blood on baboon teeth. We could see an occasional baboon flipped high into the air. But we could barely see the gorilla, he was so covered with the torment of assailing baboons.

"Come back! Godzilla!" called Jacko.

The smothering pile of baboons had stopped the great ape's step by step progress toward Elvis. I now understood that Godzilla was trying to make his way to the mirror.

But the ferocity of the pack was too much. Baboons attached to shoulders and neck, Godzilla stumbled to his knees. If the gorilla went entirely down, I knew the pack would have him.

"Come back, Godzilla!" I called. And then Kory was calling as well.

As we yelled, the great ape turned to look our way. We waved frantically for his return. He shook his head. He struggled once more to his feet. Still fighting, clubbing, and tearing under a blanket of struggling baboons, Godzilla took several more steps toward Elvis and the cavern holding the mirror.

It was then that Elvis leapt from his high perch and came down on the gorilla's head. Godzilla wobbled, then went down.

"Pack up! Pack up!" screamed Elvis, biting furiously, "Now we have him, kill this ape!"

With renewed energy and fury, their leader among them, the pack bent to the task and began pulling great swatches of black fur from the fallen ape.

Then the mouths of the pack were all blood.

"They're killing him!" Kory screamed in rage, racing back toward the wall. I caught her tail and pulled mightily to keep her from jumping into the moat.

"We must go," commanded Jacko. And without further protest, the squirrel monkeys, Kory, and I raced after Jacko into and through the garden shed, and back, in one long sprint, to the primate house.

Chapter 96

"They killed Godzilla!" cried Kory aloud.

Our little war party was panting in recovery in Jacko's cage. Fortunately, astral day was nearly done, and we felt safe from baboon pursuers. When dawn came they could not leave their enclosures anymore than any other zoo animal.

"Don't worry," said Jacko, "That old warrior will be back. The pack killed him. But as an astral animal, he died before they could show him the mirror. He will be back tomorrow with the dawn of astral day."

I felt a great relief that Godzilla was not gone for good. He had been shredded by the pack, as with incredible courage he had fought to reach the mirror. I shuddered now to think of what he had undergone in that nightmare defeat. Entirely surrounded by biting fangs!

The baboon pack no doubt was now gnawing and playing with his bones.

Kory and I looked grim.

"Don't worry, he will be back," said Jacko.

Then the old orang straightened some, "But now, the pack is after us. We must plan what to do."

Chapter 97

Kory in her anger, ranted that we should get the big animals, elephants and hippos and go over there the next night and squash every one of those baboons flat.

"Then we can break the mirror."

I didn't say that, of course, any baboon we killed that way would reappear the next day.

Jacko shook his head, "No, they will certainly hide it in a new place. They know we saw it. They won't keep it in the same place. Or worse, they might bring out the mirror and use it on us. Remember we surprised them, and in their surprise they forgot to use the mirror. But had they, I fear Godzilla would be truly sleeping now toward death."

We all sat silent a moment. We seemed to have no ideas.

Kory jumped up, "Well, I'm going to do something about this. Even if I have to sneak back into that stinking pit and break the mirror myself."

"You wouldn't!" I said. "You saw what happened to Godzilla."

"I'm a leaper, rockthrower. They won't catch me."

I shook my head unconvinced.

Jacko shook his head as well.

"No, Kory, that would be dangerous. We need to think of something else."

Just then pale pink light began breaking into the high monkey house windows. It was time for we astral beings to return to our bodies.

"What shall we do?" I said in desperation.

Jacko thought and said, "They saw us. They know who we are. Therefore, we are in danger. Until we have a better plan, I think it would be wise to sleep in our bodies by day, and stay awake by night. Sleep only in the last hour of astral day so that we might meet."

The inside of the monkey house was beginning to glow pink with dawn.

Jacko and the terrified squirrel monkeys disappeared. Then Kory said with venom, "but I'm going to do something!" as she dematerialized like ice into hot water.

I awoke in my rockthrower cage. I felt feverish and my stomach upset as if I'd been participating in my worst nightmare.

Arkteepa seemed very far away.

Chapter 98

That day I dozed and padded nervously around my cage. Every once in a while I would look across to Jacko's cage where the old orange ape was sitting with his head huddled in his arms.

I could tell he was trying to rest up.

But I was nervous and could not.

The zoo day passed eternally slow.

Chapter 99

The last visitor ambled away. The light was dimming in the monkey house. Where normally I looked forward to nightfall with all my heart, the chance to be with Kory and range free in the playgrounds of the astral zoo, now I awaited darkness with some dread. I had a queasy feeling of not knowing what was ahead.

I looked across the way as the primate house dipped into darkness. Jacko signaled me to stay awake. If we did not dream, the baboons could not surprise us.

I padded quietly in my cage through the darkness waiting for the last hour when we could meet.

It was a long cold night.

Finally, at the last hour, Jacko signaled me to sleep. I went to my corner and put my head down in my own arms.

Chapter 100

"Where is Kory?" I asked as I entered Jacko's cage.

Jacko shook his head, the wispy orange hair wavering under his chin.

"I don't know," said Jacko, "But Tip, I am worried about her. The flame of her anger burns too bright."

I nodded.

"I understand this," I said, "You see Kory, all her life she has lived in a cage. Her cage is all she has. And now someone is messing that cage up. She can't allow that. If all you have is a cage, and the cage is being wrecked, then your rage is great. Especially when she has seen a new thing within that cage, especially after living in the astral zoo."

"This is a dangerous time for her."

Again I nodded.

"Do you know what we should do about the mirror?" I asked.

"I have been thinking, yes. I've been thinking about what happened before the breaking of the last mirror."

"I'll go get Kory," I said. I turned to leave Jacko's cage.

"Be careful," I heard the old ape call behind me.

Chapter 101

"Kory?" I called as I entered her cage. I looked around at the small space filled with swing vines, ropes actually hung from bare branches, leafy plants in carefully hidden pots, a pool of water, cold and still. Kory's body was sleeping on a burlap bag crammed into a far corner.

Unlike the white walls of my carefully tiled cage, Kory's cage walls were dim grey cement. Perhaps the zookeepers knew so little about her they couldn't even fake an environment.

But Kory wasn't here. I became worried.

I left the primate house and with some caution made my way across the zoo to Kory's favorite haunt in the eucalyptus grove. I climbed the tallest tree only to find Kory's nest empty. She was nowhere in the high boughs.

I climbed to the top branch and called:

"Kory, Kory, Kory
Where are you?
Please return."

As I looked out from the highest limb, I saw the entire animal park had a solemn aspect. No animals had come out to play. No hoots, shrieks, or caws filled the playgrounds. I saw no animals wrestling on the greens, no trunks raising to pick the rich summer leaves, no scurry of the little ones in the old games of hide and seek. No growls or barks of delight.

And there in the distance was the darkened pile of the baboon heap.

And I knew I must go there.

After several minutes, I had loped across the zoo grounds. I had seen few animals other than birds on the way.

And then I found her. I was stealthily approaching the baboon heap, looking about for any ambush, when I saw Kory. She was lying down in front of the heap. I rushed out from the bushes to her.

"Kory?" I called as I ran up and squatted beside her.

But as I looked down, I could see she had been bitten here and there, and she wasn't moving. Her eyes were closed, her mouth open.

I put my nose to her nose.

Kory was asleep.

I looked at Kory's wounds, the intolerable tooth marks of the baboons.

I put my head back and howled in pain.

Chapter 102

"It's Kory," I said to Jacko. With one look at my face, Jacko understood what I meant.

"Kory? They caught her?"

I nodded.

Jacko sat down on the floor of his cage in heap. He shook his head.

"These baboons, they are such a great evil."

"They bit her!" I said, "They hurt her before they showed her the mirror." I felt my tail twitching angrily.

Jacko nodded.

"We must do it now," said Jacko. He was frowning intensely. When he turned his bright black eyes toward me I saw they were fiercely set.

"We must break mirror."

"Remember, if they used the mirror, Kory is only asleep," said Jacko.

"If we break the mirror in time, she will wake."

"You and I, go to the heap?" I said.

Jacko turned toward me and shook his head ruefully.

"No," he said, "I think you will go alone."

Chapter 103

"Tell me what I should do," I said.

"I can't tell you exactly what to do," said Jacko. "I can only tell you what I know of how the last mirror was broken. Perhaps from that we can find the way. Perhaps we can find a way to look at the mirror and not be harmed. And then a way to break it."

"How was the last mirror broken?" I asked.

"It was broken by a white monkey," said Jacko. "I was told that in a time of great trouble, in the time of the last mirror, he left the zoo for help."

"He left the zoo? How? No animal can do that," I said.

"Oh, yes," replied Jacko, "Long ago, two animals indeed escaped the zoo, the fiercest and most cunning. They escaped, and now live beyond the boundaries of the zoo fences. And the White monkey, too, he went to them for help, to learn how to break the mirror."

"What secret did he learn from them?" I asked.

Jacko shrugged, "I don't know. I only know that on returning from visiting these animals, animals that lived in complete liberty outside of the zoo, the White monkey came back and was able to destroy the mirror. These animals had taught him something which stopped the mirror from harming him."

"What animals?"

"One is a tiger, who escaped over the fence of the zoo one night, escaped and was never caught. The zookeepers tried to keep it hushed until the tiger was caught, and then when he wasn't, they've kept it a secret ever since. I'm told he still lives and hunts down among the houses by ocean. The other is a great black snake, who also escaped the zoo."

From my face Jacko could see that I was not at all happy about the prospect of calling on a tiger and a black snake, hated enemies and eaters of monkeys.

"It is extremely dangerous, but the White monkey went to them, and so you must go. I see no other way to learn the secret of the mirror."

"Why is it so dangerous, if I go as an astral being?" I said.

"Because you can't go to the tiger as an dream animal. When you go to the tiger's den, you must go in your real body. You must physically leave your cage and go out of the zoo to find him. You must leap the last fence in the darkness of night, and follow the creek to the ocean, and then in darkness and at low tide, look for his prints in the sand, they will lead you to his lair. You must enter his lair and face him. And there, of course, you may die."

"And this snake, where does he live? Must I go to him in my jungle body as well?"

"No, the great black snake, he lives close by. He lives beneath the zoo. You can go to him in your astral being. But it makes no difference. When you go to see this snake, astral being or not, the old one told me, if the black snake eats you, you stay eaten. You die."

"What am I to learn from these animals?" I asked.

Jacko shook his head slowly. He didn't know.

Then I tried to muster a smile.

"So, if I'm to leave the zoo, how do I get out?"

Jacko nodded that I had accepted this journey into darkness.

He bid me follow and then disappeared through the wall of his cage.

We two lone primates walked quietly through the bushes of the lower grounds. We went to the far reaches of the zoo where the last cyclone fence stood.

"There, you must go beyond that fence. And then," said Jacko, "follow the creek to the ocean. Once at the ocean, go to the lowest water mark at low tide. You'll find paw prints leading away. Follow those."

"Now come," he said. He turned and began lumbering away again.

I followed for several minutes until we came back to the plaza before the primate house.

"It's here," said Jacko. "No one else knows this, but it is here." Jacko pointed at the ground.

I looked down to see a metal manhole cover at my feet.

"That is where the black snake lives."

I frowned deeply.

"Long ago he escaped and went to live in the tunnels below the zoo. You must go down there and find him. You must go to the last light, and a little farther."

I swallowed. No tree-living monkey, no sun-loving monkey from Arkteepa ever wanted to go into caverns below ground. My very nature rebelled at the thought.

I sat staring at the forbidding home of a black snake.

"This is hard," I said.

Jacko nodded.

"But how do I get out of my cage?" I turned to ask.

"Come," said Jacko, and with that he climbed the drain spout, hand over hand, to the top of the primate house. I bound and followed him up.

We crossed the roof until we stopped before one of the sealed skylights that hung over each animal cage.

"This is your cage," said Jacko. He pointed a boney finger at the skylight, and then to a steel pin that held the window latched in place.

He bent, and with his teeth, he pulled the pin from the cover.

He raised the skylight cover back and forth to show me it was now open. I opened the skylight and looked down.

There was my rockthrower body sleeping below.

"I can't fit through such a window. This is why you must go alone."

"Tonight, don't sleep. Instead, you must escape through this sky window, and then first, go to the tiger's lair. Then, if you return" and Jacko looked at me to mark his concern, "the next day, we will go to see the snake," said Jacko gravely.

I nodded.

"What if they don't tell me how to break the mirror?" I asked.

"Come back to me. And I will tell you how I think it might be done. And why it must be you to do it."

Then the morning sun was rising and we had to go back to our cages.

Chapter 104

That morning, awake and starving in my cage, I watched the zookeepers enter the primate house and begin their routine cleaning. I looked over at Jacko as I saw he, too, was pressed to the glass watching them move from cage to cage.

And then a solitary zookeeper, his face a mask of discomfort, walked past our cages carrying a limp furry body in his arms.

I watched as he carried Kory out of the primate house.

I banged my head against the glass. I clawed its smooth impenetrable surface. I howled a short howl. Then banged my face on that surface I could never reach Kory through.

Across the way, his orangutan eyes like cups of sadness, Jacko shook his head and went to sit in the corner with his back turned to me.

Chapter 105

The sun was going down. I had sat and suffered in that cage more than I could stand. The last zookeeper had left with a final click of the primate house door lock. Jacko had coached me to wait until darkness to go find a free-roaming tiger.

But I had something else to do.

I scrambled up the branches of my climbing structure. I reached out and pushed the skylight open.

Then I was up and out.

Even in my turmoil, the scent of the air on the rooftop was fresh and free. I realized I had not tasted this scent in my jungle body for more than a year. It was odd, but just the scent of freedom seemed healing.

Chapter 106

I stopped and looked down over the edge of the refuse pit. There Kory lay. It was quite hard for me to look down on her, her body cast on a heap among other dead animals. I jumped down. Then I walked slowly over to her.

She lay on her stomach, her arms and legs spread eagle over the garden refuse and zoo litter. Her eyes were closed, her mouth open barely breathing in a deep and dreamless sleep.

I grabbed her foot and began to pull. I tugged her to the edge of the pit. Then, with the help of a lone tree root, I pulled and dragged her up the earthen wall and out of the pit.

I continued dragging her by her foot and tail across the grass. I dragged and dragged her as far as I could. Finally I reached a low hanging lilac bush, shaped like an igloo, and I tugged her deep underneath it.

I left her lying unconscious under the cover of this old flowering lilac. Its branches bent low covering her, sheltering her, hidden in deeper grasses.

"Kory, I have to leave you here," I said. "But, if I can, I will come back."

I took a deep breath. And again I smelt the scent of fresh air and freedom, and behind this now, a slight scent of lilacs.

Then I left.

Left to escape the zoo.

Chapter 107

I dropped over the cyclone fence and looked around. Through a small barrier of trees and shrubs, I could see city streets and houses stretching in all directions. Though it was twilight, lamps lit many windows and pink street lights were blinking on. A small wooded creek ran behind the nearest houses, and this being the closest path that appeared to me like the jungle in the city, and the only way to the ocean, I hopped down into its brushy cover.

I scrambled down and stepped into the creek. I found the water in this creek quite shallow, nearly paper thin. Then I realized even this small run off from the zoo had a concrete base to carry the water efficiently away. This civilization was taking no chances that zoo water would run free into its ground.

I followed the creek bed, hopping from rock to rock, for nearly a mile. Darkness had fallen. Then I began to hear it; the steady drumming thump of ocean waves at night. I could smell the sea air among the brushy smells of twigs and vines.

I entered a culvert, tall enough for a man to walk through without bending, and came out the other side with my feet sinking in damp sand.

And before me, in the dark, floated rafts of white waves, rearing and rolling on the horizon.

I had reached the ocean. And in this dark, I prayed to Binah to keep me safe from her cold ocean power and might. Binah, source of all earth and ocean, keep me safely back from your great vision of cold and indifferent water. I realized a small warm-hearted monkey would be totally out of his element there among those great waters. And I must travel now down to the ocean's very edge.

To look for the paw prints in the sand.

Chapter 108

It was only minutes after reaching the packed sand at the water's edge that I found one.

A clawed paw print, as big as saucer. Then I saw a string of them leading away down the beach. This was a big animal, I could barely hop the distance from one paw print to another.

After a quarter mile of trotting in darkness along the beach, I came to another running stream. Here the water was deeper, and any paw prints placed in it quickly washed away. The prints, however, did not come out on the other side of this creek. I turned and followed the water back up toward the sand dunes and far city lights.

Then I came to a black maw open before me. Another culvert open in blackness like a huge mouth.

I sat down to stare into it. I could see nothing. I put my head within its edge and listened. And there, faintly, behind the waves' drumming and rush, I could just pick out a sound coming from deep inside the pipe. A slow intermittent rumble.

The purr of a large jungle cat.

The ancient chill of the predator went down my back. The enemy was near and my body rebelled at being there. I sniffed and indeed I caught the smell of tiger.

"Don't just stand there sniffing your death," came a low growl from the darkness. "Walk right in!"

Two red globes had lit glowing now in the darkness at me.

"Come in, don't make me run out there to kill you," laughed the deep voice in the darkness.

"Who are you?" I shouted, feeling my throat freezing up with my fear.

"I am the great unseen one, the consummate killer, the destroyer of you and all, at any time and place I choose. Does that tell you enough of what is in store for you?" said the voice pleasantly.

"You're a tiger?" I said.

"Yes, I am a tiger."

Then the two shining eyes heaved into the air, and the next instant I realized I'd been pounced up and was being carried by my tail deep into the tiger's den.

I was set down on sandy ground and a heavy paw placed on my chest to hold me down.

I screeched in fear a little. "Don't kill me, please. I didn't come here to be killed," I said.

"Quiet down now," said the great voice above me.

"I destroy anything I want," said the tiger, "And if you follow my path, sooner or later you meet me in the dark."

Chapter 109

"Don't kill me, I'm from the zoo. I need your help."

"I don't care about the zoo," said the dark voice above me. "I don't live there anymore. And I rarely go there. I live here now. Now this is my kingdom."

There was a pause. Then the voice added, "Such as it is."

"Animals are being killed in the zoo. I came to talk with you. Once a white monkey came to see you. He learned something I must learn."

"Please, I make it a habit not to talk to my food while I eat," grunted the tiger in the blackness. I could see nothing, only feel the constant heavy pressure of his paw on my chest.

Then I felt hot breath on my face.

"But a white monkey came here, and didn't die, you didn't eat him."

"You're a talkative little morsel, most animals I catch just flatten out and prepare to die. Those, of course, that see me coming."

There was a slow sniff above my face.

"You are a rockthrower," said the tiger. "I'll be. I haven't eaten one of those in years. Let's take you out and get a look at you. Then we'll eat."

I felt teeth close on my tail and I was carried hanging like an opossum upside down out of the culvert.

Outside the culvert, the stars were out and a dim moon rising behind clouds. I saw the tiger carrying me was as big as a park bench. He set me down in the sand and let me hop away a few steps.

I knew I couldn't outrun his pounce so I sat.

"Well, you are a rockthrower," said the cat.

"Yes, and I believe the white monkey was, too," I said.

"Ah, I do remember. This white monkey, he came to me. He was from my old home. He was a monkey from the temple of Arkteepa. And you're right, I did let him go. I remember. I gave him a test, and he passed, and so I told him what he wanted to know and let him go. I had never done that before. For any animal. Strange how the past always comes back to you."

And then the moon broke in a search light beam through the clouds. All the area around the jungle cat and I was illuminated with silver light.

And I saw the jungle cat before me was entirely white.

Chapter 110

"Arkteepa, Arkteepa," sighed the great cat. "It was there I hunted with pleasure. My stealth was great. The source of rockthrowers or any other animal I wanted endless. And there, after killing and eating my quarry, there before me was always the vision of Arkteepa, the golden stone temple. My beautiful ancient home."

"It was not like here," said the cat shaking its large head. "Here, young monk, I hunt in absolute secrecy. Only on the blackest of nights. I let no one see me as I wander the city streets and alleys alone. I must be careful to never step into the light. For here to be seen means live in a cage or to die."

"Now, instead of the lush jungle trails, now, I haunt back porches and alleys, deep bushes in the park. In deepest night, I hide in the shadows of garbage bins and abandoned cars, pouncing on stray cats and mongrels for my dinner. Sometimes in summer, I am able to enter open windows and kill and drag off a sleeping child. I catch an occasional teenager. I have even stooped so low as to eat a bum sleeping it off in these dunes. It is certainly not the regal hunt of a superb killer for me anymore. Disgusting and tiring is what it is."

The cat shook its head with regret.

"I, too, am from Arkteepa," I said.

The cat raised its head. "You are?"

"Yes," I said. "Like the White monkey."

"Do you know me?" asked the cat.

"Yes, you are Gabur, the great white tiger. You killed my grandfather."

"I killed your grandfather? Then you do know me! What joy, why we are almost related. This is wonderful. You are going to make quite a poignant meal. Memories, memories, memories."

"No, I need your help. Why did you let the White monkey go? I need to go back and destroy something in the zoo."

"Well, you've certainly come to the right place to learn about destruction."

"Tell me, why did you let the White monkey go?" I insisted.

"Oh," said Gabur, "I gave him a test. A test of seeing. And the lucky little rascal passed. So I helped him out with a few suggestions and let him go."

"I am a rockthrower, too. You and I lived on the same temple. Please, give me the test. Help me, too."

"Oh, I don't know. If I don't eat you, I don't see much in it for me."

"Will you promise to come back and visit me another time? Hopefully before you're too old and stringy?"

He was asking me to accept to come back and be destroyed.

"Yes," I said. Then I hastily added, "Someday."

"Good," said Gabur. "But if you fail the test, then I eat you now anyway."

I gulped and said, "Okay."

Gabur nodded. He got up and paced back and forth in the moonlight.

"Look at me, rockthrower. What do you see? I am your old nemesis from the jungle. I am the hated one. And here, even here on the edge of the ocean, I am hated. I must walk the water line so that my paw prints are never found. I live in shadows. I am never seen. I never ever roar my superb roar before I kill anymore. My pounce and kill is hidden, not done in jungle freedom. I, the best of the jungle hunters, am forgotten and unseen. The animal folk around me don't know my power. They only know me in the surprise of their death struggle and dying. And it is my job to kill and kill any in my way. Look at me!"

As the cat talked, I watched the large sleek animal's pacing. His white, striped bulk shone silver in the moonlight. The power and drive within his skin, shining from his eyes was unearthly and intense. Then Gabur came round and walked up to me.

His face, his finger-length fangs, were inches from my head.

"So here is your test, rockthrower. Look at me and tell me: Which of the following statements is correct?

"A, I am all powerful and to be worshipped."

"B, I am beautiful."

"C, I am going to kill you and gnaw your bones."

"D, All of the above."

I was so frightened of the beast so near me, I could barely keep my eyes from closing. I stiffened my heart and looked up. And I saw an old jungle cat standing alone, shining white in the moonlight.

"B, you are Gabur and you are beautiful."

The cat looked down on me. Then a tear slowly slipped from its eye.

"Yes, little monk, that is the right answer."

Chapter 111

The white tiger's loneliness stood out so plainly before me.

"Do you really see my beauty?" asked the tiger somewhat hesitantly.

"Yes," I said, "You too are from Arkteepa."

"That is the right answer. You've looked into the face of destruction and seen the beauty beyond. You have passed the test."

"I do rather wish I was there once more. In the jungle, near our ancient home. I get a bit sick of killing alley cats. Have you ever eaten a skunk? Man, that's an ordeal. Sometimes, you know, the jungle calls back to me. And then it is all I can do to keep going. Keep destroying."

"Why do you?" I said, "Keep destroying?"

"Monk, come now. That is my function. I wander the jungle trails, eating my fill. I'm meant to kill those things that have lost their power or usefulness. That are sick or have wandered stupidly beyond the tribe. Every jungle needs its tiger."

I cleared my throat to get back to business.

"The zoo. I come from the zoo. There the baboons are killing us. They have a weapon. A mirror. I have to break it. Can you help me?"

"I used to enjoy killing baboons quite a bit," grunted Gabur. "However, I never go back to the zoo unless I have to. I'm a real animal. I don't need to travel in my astral body anymore. I don't think I want to go back to the zoo, even if it is to slay a tribe of boons."

"Okay, don't come to the zoo then. But I need to break the mirror. I don't know how. How do I destroy it?"

The great white tiger raised its chin in thought.

"Little monk, you already know how. Look in the face of destruction and see beyond. If you look into the mirror and don't see the beauty beyond it, then you become what you are trying to destroy. To destroy what needs to be destroyed, with a tiger's heart look through it, to the beauty of the thing you want beyond. Then you can destroy the thing before you."

"With a tiger's heart, look through the mirror?"

"Yes, to the thing you want, the thing you want with all your heart."

"What is that?" I asked.

"Why, little monk," grunted Gabur with mild humor, "That is Arkteepa."

Chapter 112

"How will that destroy the mirror?" I asked.

"Look, I don't have all the answers," said the tiger, "Now, go little monk, and destroy your mirror. Before I decide to eat you now."

I turned to leave.

"And remember your promise," said the tiger's voice behind me, "You will come back and see my beauty again. Someday."

A last charge of fear raised the hackles on my shoulders. And then I scampered away into the dark.

Chapter 113

Exhausted, I pulled myself back over the cyclone fence and dropped into the zoo. I made my way back across the playground, the concessions area, to the still building of the primate house. I never believed that I would be glad to reach it, but I was. I wearily shinnied up the drain spout even as I heard the first zookeepers scuffing the ground with their brooms that morning. I quickly crossed the roof, found my open skylight, and drop down inside my cage.

Jacko was asleep across the way in his cage. He was asleep with his face on the glass facing me. I figured he had been waiting for my return, but weariness had taken the old ape, as now he dozed against the glass. So I, too, returned to my corner and slept.

Chapter 114

Later that day, when I woke around noon, I got up and trotted to the pane at the front of my cage. I looked to see what Jacko was doing, to signal him that my visit to Gabur's lair had been a success. I was surprised to see Jacko still sleeping against the glass.

A half hour later, a blue suited zookeeper entered his cage and pushed him with a broom handle. The old ape fell over.

It took four zookeepers to lug the sleeping orangutan by his arms and legs out of the cage.

Before Jacko finally departed, several of the zookeepers looked over their shoulders to see why the little monkey was screeching so across the way.

Chapter 115

Now I knew that I had to go see the great black snake beneath the zoo tonight. Alone.

Chapter 116

I went to the round manhole cover sitting like a target in the middle of the zoo plaza. I sat looking down at it a moment, uneasy about going down into the unknown.

I expected there was nothing really pleasant waiting for me down there. There in the forgotten turnings and twistings of the sewer passages under the zoo. Down where the refuse and waste of our above-ground life went.

And here, into this vile darkness, I must now tread. Tread to find the very nemesis of my tribe, a black snake, eater of monkeys. Killer of hoppers, leapers, and rockthrowers alike.

I shivered.

It was only my great unhappiness that forced me to go down.

Unless I did, there was little chance of joy, freedom, or being with Kory and Jacko ever again.

Any monkey who saw my face would have seen my mouth rumpled with great distaste. They might have laughed had they not known what I was facing. In my heart, I was facing blackness itself.

I began lowering myself into the manhole, through the heavy plate cover. Soon I was hanging by my fingertips like a monkey on a branch. I gulped.

Then I let go.

Chapter 117

I hit mushy sludge with a splash.

"Yuck," I thought, feeling the stuff squeeze up between my toes. I was ankle deep.

"I don't want to be here," I said out loud to Jacko.

"Of course, you don't. Now get on with it. Quit feeling sorry for yourself!" I heard my own mind answer.

All around me were dark, dank walls of grey stone, black and mossed over with molds and fungus. The tunnel was dark, but there, some fifty feet away, I could see a distant glow and a small snake-like reflection of light wavering eerily on the stream surface.

I walked unhappily, my tail up high with disgust, toward this light.

After a minute of walking that seemed endless, I came to where the tunnel turned, and on rounding the corner, I saw several lights, burning dimly, stationed about fifty yards apart, hanging from the tunnel ceiling. Each light put down a grey spot on the tunnel floor, followed by darkness again until reaching the next light some distance down the passage.

"Go to the last light and then a little further," I heard Jacko's voice say in my mind.

Slowly, I followed the lights, one after another, through light and dark, down the long tunnel.

I felt relief whenever I entered a light. But my loneliness was great whenever I reentered the darkness.

Something bumped into and jumped over my foot.

I lurched back to see a rat, nose wriggling, look up at me surprised then flee.

As my eyes adjusted, I could now see rats running on ledges, overhanging pipes, and narrow tunnels sidetracking off from the main passage. I shuddered. I'd never cared for anything with hairless tails. Their occasional squeaks in the distance were like fingernails scraped on chalkboard.

I didn't want to watch rats so I stepped warily onward.

The tunnel became colder as I passed each light. Finally, after many minutes of travel, to God knows where under the zoo, I saw up ahead there was only one light. A single light burning weakly, needing to be changed soon, wavering a bit like a candle.

Beyond that was only darkness.

I reached and stood under the last pale light.

"Hello!" I shouted. But there was no sound, no answer.

"To the last light, and a little further," I heard again in my mind.

I sighed. I kind of wished I could just stick around under this light. The blackness rested there mercilessly before me.

I had to go into it. My only consolation was that others, another monkey had gone into this darkness before me and survived. And that now was my only hope.

I began feeling my way into the black. I had no destination, other than taking one step at a time, my foot placed with painful unknowing out in front of me.

I soon was in complete darkness when I heard a worrisome rustling up ahead.

"Hello, any snakes up there? Got some time for a short visit?" I said, trying to muster some humor.

And then two green glowing beads appeared in the dark. They stared unblinking at me. Then they slowly and silently rose toward the tunnel ceiling.

I felt a shiver of fear streak down my spine. Something was up ahead and had seen me.

I stood still, trembling, and looked at the great green eyes, glowing incandescently in the dark. And then I made out something else. Another glowing, a purplish aura, floating above the ghastly eyes that pierced me.

And this second glow was the shape of a lily.

Chapter 118

"Hello, anybody there?" I called into the dark, after swallowing my fear.

"Yes, pork chop, I am," said a low hissing voice. It had said this with a certain grim humor, but the glowing eyes had not wavered upon me in the least.

"I, I have to talk to you," I said, unsure if I had anything to say at all. "It's about the zoo. Things have happened there. I need to know what to do."

"Do you mind if I just eat you first?" said the black voice.

The two glowing eyes lowered slightly, pushing ahead about a foot in my direction.

"How about we talk, then eat?" I said. I was at a loss for words, and so was ready to say anything that came into my head.

"Ha, good one," said the dark voice with some mirth. "You could be an amusing morsel. Yes, let's take it in that order."

I heard a great rustling that seemed to fill the entire tunnel around me. I was startled. Whatever was ahead of me was huge.

Then before I noticed that the glowing eyes had disappeared, I was picked up by the scruff of the neck as easily as a mother cat picks up one of her litter. Dangling helplessly, I felt myself transported back through the blackness to the very edge of grey light shed by the last overhead bulb.

I was put down fully exposed in the grey circle. I looked up to see a giant snake's head, larger than a bucket, withdraw into the darkness above me.

I have to say by now I was one little pretty freaked out monkey.

Chapter 119

"Now my little snack, what brings you here with such revulsion for me so plainly on your snout?"

The voice that had said this came straight from the blackness. I could not see the great snake before me.

"There are deaths in the zoo," I said. "Animals, they fall asleep, then are thrown out to die."

"A mirror?" said voice.

"Yes," I nodded.

"So what?" said the bodiless voice, "deaths occur in the zoo all the time. That is upstairs, above me, so let it happen. Why do you think that concerns me? I who rule and govern all from below. I've been known to kill a few zoo folks myself."

"An old orang, Jacko, told me of you, that you might help."

"Why did he think that?" hissed the voice.

"Because you helped a white monkey once," I said. "And according to Jacko, he returned to the zoo and was able to break a mirror."

"Oh, nonsense," laughed the voice, "No white monkey ever returned from here."

After short pause, the black voice said.

"Will you be my slave?"

I stared not knowing what to answer.

"I need help, for the zoo," I said.

"Nonsense, you must first help yourself. For example, blackness and unspeakable horror sit coiled before you. Wouldn't you say it's you that needs the help?"

A large snake's head slowly began to form, a grey image pushing my way out of the darkness. Its green eyes lit, staring dangerously at me.

"After all, it's you I'm looking at. Who cares about your little zoo."

I stood silent before the slowly approaching head. I knew I was being stalked.

"Why don't you escape, run away, if the zoo bothers you? Go back to your homeland."

"My homeland? Arkteepa?" I said, "It is too far...but certainly, I wish—"

"You are from Arkteepa?" exclaimed the snake. The serpent raised its head in surprise. It stood above me in the shadows, looking down at me, as its forked tongue, thick as a garden hose, ran speculatively in and out of its mouth.

"You are a monk from the temple of Arkteepa?" asked the great snake. "A rockthrower?"

"Yes," I said.

"Well, amazing! My goodness! Arkteepa was my temple, and its monkeys were my tribe. I am Kunda, your master. I'm the great black snake that scared the living daylights out of the rockthrowers at the temple. At least, until I was caught and carried away to that zoo."

A certain bitter venom had entered the snake's voice.

"You are Kunda? The feared dark being from within the temple?" I said incredulous.

"Yes," said the snake with a gratified nod. "And you are one of my own."

I stood looking up at the great snake with unbelieving eyes.

"Here, I'll prove it to you," hissed the snake.

Its head lowered in the darkness and there I saw a purple shining, the shape of a flower, glowing intensely before me from the snake's head.

"That," said the great snake, "is the Great Lily."

Chapter 120

"The White monkey and Kunda both came here to this zoo?" I said.

"I expect we were both grabbed the same night, but that was years and years ago. I was probably only a mere 25 feet long back then; now, by the way, I'm a healthy 45 feet and still growing," a note of pride had entered the snake's voice.

"But you said the White monkey never came here!" I said.

"No, I said the White monkey never returned from here," corrected the great snake.

"I don't understand," I said.

"Let's just say he didn't leave here the White monkey. He didn't leave here the same white monkey that came in."

"Why?"

"Because he left here knowing he was my servant."

"But you helped him?"

"I don't know. He came here and found the truth. I don't know if the truth helps anybody."

"He was able to break the mirror, according to Jacko," I said.

"Is that so?" asked Kunda, coiling a bit nearer with interest.

"Yes," I said as confidently as I could.

"Then, perhaps you should be my servant, too?" the snake laughed, "Or perhaps you should be a little rockthrower sandwich. I haven't had one of those in just ages."

I gulped. "I have to say, I don't care much for you eating-small-animals jokes," I said.

"The pleasure is all mine," stated Kunda regally.

"The zoo is dying. I need your help, Kunda. Your secret. Jacko told me that it could help me break the mirror. Will you tell me?"

"I only tell that to my slaves," said Kunda with a refusing shake of his head.

"I must be your slave to learn it?"

"Yessss."

"The White monkey, to learn your secret, he became your slave?"

"Let's not talk about him," said the snake, "Let's talk about you. What flavor are you, exactly? You're not one of those licorice-tasting monkeys, are you? I remember now that rockthrowers used to have the most delicious musty flavor."

Kunda's eyes closed with remembered pleasure.

"I haven't had a rockthrower....not since I escaped the zoo and came to live here in eternal blackness."

"Kunda, help me. The White monkey. What did he have to do for you to help him? I will do it, too. Jacko told me that the White monkey went to see Gabur to learn how to destroy the mirror, then he came to you."

"I too have gone to Gabur, the killing white tiger, and he has told me his secret."

"Gabur? You went to see Gabur, and lived?" asked Kunda.

I nodded.

"Fascinating!"

I could hear Kunda's huge body coiling with interest in the dark.

"How is that old rascal?" asked Kunda.

"Lonely, as a beautiful killer can be," I said.

"Yes, yes," nodded Kunda. "Gabur, I always liked him for his determined spirit for killing. I admired his merciless techniques. Though he and I are different, much different in our ways."

"He told me that to break a mirror, you must look through it with a tiger's heart. You must look through it and see what you want."

"And does that break it?" inquired Kunda mildly.

I hesitated. "No, I don't think so," I admitted.

"Good! That shows you are not an imbecile! Perhaps you can eventually break the mirror. Assuming first I don't smother you in chocolate sauce and have you as a little monkey sundae."

Kunda began to laugh a belly-laugh, an enormous coiled writhing, which was a terrible sight in a great snake.

"A little human humor there," said Kunda, straightening himself out a bit with a wistful smile.

"I ate one once."

"You ate a human?" I said, shocked.

"Yes, he squiggle quite a bit, but I finally got him down. The hard hat was the hardest part. The boots also have a particularly greasy flavor."

I grimaced.

"And, of course, I nearly choked on the flashlight," snorted the snake.

"Kunda, I need to know about the White monkey!" I said in an accusing tone.

Kunda flared his green eyes and stared irritably down at me.

Chapter 121

"The White Monkey? Oh, him," said Kunda.

"He had to accept me into his life. Accept me, the blackness, the dark being who rules. He had to accept me, my power, the only real power to have affect on the world."

"And let me tell you, that little squirt didn't want to. He was a stubborn monk," Kunda chuckled to himself.

"But you see, no matter how lily white you are, I cannot be ignored. It took him a long time, and a lot of terror to accept me, to accept that he was my servant."

Kunda's mouth rippled in satisfied remembrance.

"My slave," he hissed to himself.

"Kunda, why is this?" I asked shivering before this great black animal, an animal that lived alone, in darkness, in the depths. "Why must I or the White monkey return to you, serve you? The world is large, filled with light! I can roam free. Do as I will. All without you."

"You free? No! The truth is, you live in the zoo! You live only as an astral being, asleep. Get with it, chump," laughed Kunda.

"And as long as you are asleep and you don't know about me, I rule you."

"Without me, without my power that I bestow, you never build a nest, you never make the catch that ends your quest. Gabur, yes, he is beautiful, he can destroy. He knows the beauty of destruction. Once you know his secret, then you have the power to destroy. Once you know mine, you can build," Kunda's snake tongue licked out at me several times like a forked conductor's wand moving at a happy beat.

"You can also have a lot of fun."

"What did the White monkey do? How did he learn your secret?"

"He accepted me. And I accepted him as one of my animals. And, of course, then I marked him. Marked him here with my beautiful lily."

Kunda lowered his head so that I saw the bright glowing mark on his forehead.

"And he had to accept, coming down here, into the darkness and dirt of my home, that he could no longer be the White monkey."

"From that day on, he was the Gray monkey."

"He changed color. Here in your cave?" I asked.

"Yessss, sort of like a beauty parlor, aye?" laughed Kunda, "A white monkey came here, a gray monkey left."

"But his sacrifice, it allowed him to leave here alive and to break the mirror," stated Kunda.

The point of decision had come to me.

"I must accept you, too?" I asked.

Kunda laughed, his tail rolling like a fire hose.

"You! You cannot deny me! You are my little Arkteepan monk. You serve me whether you know it or not. Arkteepa, it is so far away...You and I miss it, we do...So every once in a while, I go back. I go back to the closest thing to it: the zoo."

"The zoo animals don't know about you. They don't know you come there," I said.

"They should, little monk," laughed Kunda. "It's dangerous for them, if they don't."

Kunda opened his mouth wide. There hanging in the air, over my head, was the great white mouth of a killer snake. It hung over me like a bell, Kunda giving me no choice but to see it.

I grimaced. I had gotten the message.

As long as the zoo animals didn't know of Kunda, then he could steal into the zoo and take anyone he wanted.

"But," chuckled Kunda, "Normally, I don't go there. It's not an environment I like to slide through. It's also difficult dragging struggling animals out through the bars of their cages."

Kunda looked around him at the walls of his black cave, lit dimly by the failing bulb of the last sewer system light.

"Did you know that rats come in ten flavors?" said Kunda.

I shook my head.

"They do, I prefer the turkey-flavored ones the best. You can actually learn to tell the flavors apart. So you see, even old Kunda, and his beautiful blackness, King, Emperor, and Master of the dark, Master of the underworld, the underworld that supports your zoo, even he gets a little lazy at times."

Kunda laughed silently to himself, his mouth open like a cat trying to cough up a furball.

The Kunda's head turned to me. It was the sullen direct look of a predator at its prey.

I shivered.

"So. Do you accept me? To learn my secret, to break the mirror? Or, do you die here unknowing? Tell me, you little turkey-flavored monkey."

"I have a choice?" I asked, having nothing better to say.

"No," said Kunda. And he gave me a slow snaky smile.

"What if I accept you now and then refuse you later?" I asked.

"Then, as I do for all animals that refuse to give me my due, I come and get them in the zoo. They become my servant or my lunch."

"How can I become a servant to evil?" I cried.

At that Kunda's head bucked back and he reeled as if struck.

"Monk, you do not understand me. So you insult! That is the most dangerous thing you can do, here, in my complete power."

The snake frowned angrily at me. Its eyes were trained into mine.

"I am not evil. That is only what the animals that I'm forced to eat think. I am the force of life itself. Oh no, I am needed. I am an undeniable and essential part. It is my will the comes up out of the mire and drives you to do what you do. It is my energy that supplies you with your Self, that allows you to create! To make your nests, to create you meager little family! My blackness guards the source from which you spring, you live upon my temple. You eat my temple's fruit! And I..." smiled Kunda, "am a large part of your life. I am a large part of the song. I give you a hint there...But I am not evil! Only bird brains attach good or evil to animals."

"But what about a baboon like Elvis, isn't he evil?" I asked.

"Yes, I know Elvis. He is an animal gone wrong. But I don't think of him as evil." Kunda smiled to himself. Then he laughed.

"I like to think of him as a snack."

Then Kunda looked again at me.

"So my little rockthrower. What will it be? Accept me or die?"

I thought of Kory and Jacko sleeping toward death. I nodded.

"I accept."

"Good," said Kunda, and he smiled his eerie snake smile again, "I assume you have chosen as you have because you have work to do. Good! Let's get on with it."

"You can always be a little monkey sandwich later."

Chapter 122

"So, Kunda," I said, "What is your secret?"

"My secret, little brother," said Kunda, "Is that I am here to tell you something you cannot ignore. Binah, Great Mother earth, is your mother. And Binah is my mother, too. I, in my beauty and blackness, am your brother. I am part of every animal in the zoo. You belong to me, and I belong to you."

"What?" I said. Hearing this monster declare that it was my brother was a lot to gulp.

"And the black light that lights my underground world here," continued Kunda, glancing at the cobwebbed ceiling, the damp slime-molds about him, "is as important as the great light that Keth carries over your world each day. Binah's black light shines up from the earth and is equal to Keth's shining down. It is Keth's light that shines down upon you as you sit trapped in your cages in the zoo. And at night, it is Binah's great light that shines upon you when you leave your bodies and travel in the astral zoo. It is Binah's light that creates your astral day."

"You see, we are not enemies," said Kunda proudly. "We are just all part of the same jungle. We all abide the same jungle law. Yet, because you are masters of Keth's light, you leave me down here alone."

"Animals think I'm evil. Ha!" snorted Kunda, "I'm not. I'm just a great snake. Perhaps the greatest black snake, most charming there is, a cute little squirmer as my mother used to say," Kunda chuckled, "—that was before I became 45 feet long, but I live under Keth's light and within Binah's light, too. "

"And, of course, sometimes those animals tick me off, and so I eat them, big deal." Kunda's head and neck lowered in a shrug.

"I belong to you, you belong to me?" I said.

"I am you and you are me," confirmed Kunda, "the same, always the same under Keth's strong light or Binah's shining darkness."

"And so, monkey brother, that's my secret."

"How is that going to help me break the mirror?" I asked.

"In this way: Gabur is right. He has told you the secret to destruction is to look through the mirror and see the thing you want. See Arkteepa, shining before you in both lights. See my temple calling out to you in both its light and darkness, you who should live on its golden steps. See through the mirror, beyond to the thing you desire to create. And then, remember me, and sing the song. Sing the song of the Great Lily. As you gaze upon this temple and sing my song, you will be able to destroy the mirror."

"But how?" I asked.

"I can't tell you exactly. It is a great mystery. Sing the song and a great mystery will happen. It will happen like lightening. Like a path to follow to Arkteepa. It will allow you to break the mirror."

I couldn't fathom how singing a song would break this mirror.

"I won't die?" I said.

Kunda lowered his head again and shrugged.

"You may die," said Kunda, "Nothing is certain."

I nodded and turned to go.

"Wait!" hissed the great snake. I turned back to find the face hung just above me.

Kunda lowered his great head, showing the purple glowing lily upon his pate. Then his forehead punched my chest. I tottered back and nearly fell down.

I looked down on my bruised chest to now see a big purple lily on my fur. I wiped at it, but it wouldn't come off.

"There," smiled Kunda, "now I have marked you. You are my servant. I can recognize you in any darkness, in any light."

I looked at my chest shining with this glowing lily.

"Good-bye, my Arkteepan monk, my slave," hissed the now disembodied voice in the dark. I could hear a great rustling flowing away down the sewer tunnel.

Troubled, I turned to go back to the zoo.

Chapter 123

I crawled out of the manhole and headed back toward my cage in the primate house. It was near dawn and I was exhausted. I needed to return to my sleeping body to rest. The astral light would soon be waning, like a translucent rainbow colored curtain coming down, as the brilliant sun rose over skyscrapers in the East.

I thought of going to check Kory's sleeping body under the lilacs, but there was not enough time. Any minute now, the first zookeeper would begin walking between the zoo buildings, a lonely sentinel carrying a broom.

"Get that rat skin," someone shouted behind me.

Six baboons bound out of the surrounding bushes beside the primate house. Their teeth were bared and their eyes bright with hate as they charged me. I ducked down and looked for an escape route.

And then I felt paws fall hard on my back.

I rolled over and kicked, only to find Buck's yellow eyes staring down at me, his mouth bent in a malignant smile.

Twice as big as I, his four paws each pinned one of my legs to the ground. On my back, helpless, I tried to gnaw at his paws to force an escape.

"Well, tick bait," said Buck, "We meet again."

Then Buck bent down and bit me on the shoulder, so hard that I felt bones crunch.

I screamed.

The other baboons were now crowded shoulder to shoulder around Buck pinning his victim.

My pain and terror were great.

"Let me bite his tail right off," I heard in Randall's voice.

The other baboons around him laughed.

"No, I'm just going to tear it off, right now," said Buck. He grinned down on me.

I took several more bites at Buck's paw to no effect. Buck simply batted my face with his hand which jarred me with pain from my wounded shoulder. I could now see my own blood on Buck's teeth as he smiled down at me.

"Back!" I heard shouted from somewhere. Nearly twenty baboons had gathered around us now.

I realized then that Elvis had come on the scene. He was somewhere behind Buck.

"Make way," I heard Elvis shout, "I've got a little mirror I want to show to an ugly ugly monkey!"

The surrounding crowd of baboons laughed and hee-hawed.

I was some kind of fun spectacle to them.

Then Elvis appeared behind Buck's shoulder. Cradled in one hand was a gleaming object with four perfectly straight sides. Elvis roared to set his playmates back from him. His yellow teeth had flashed like fang-shaped candles.

The baboon crowd made way.

Elvis nipped Buck's back, and Buck, startled, jumped off me. I lay on my back, hurt and exhausted on the ground, staring up at Elvis. The repulsion on Elvis' face was easy to read as he looked down on me.

"I have something for you to see," sneered Elvis.

Elvis' baboon mane was wide like a cobra's and his hackles up. "It's called a mirror. Something beyond your puny monkey mind. Don't you wish now you were a wondrous baboon such as we?" taunted Elvis. More laughter rose from the baboons.

He was going to turn the mirror on me and I wasn't prepared to break it.

"Nothing to say?" asked Elvis. The baboon leader had squatted now beside me, calmly holding the glass in his lap. He was close enough that I could see fleas rippling over his nearly bald belly.

"Nothing to say about Jacko, or your little bag of female shit, Kory?"

I sat up and bared my teeth. I growled. If ever I felt it, it was now I felt ready to kill.

"Ha!" called Elvis, "this little monkey thinks he's a tiger! Well, he's not a tiger. No, no, no." Elvis laughed. "You are not even close to being a baboon! We, the wondrous ones, will soon show you that. You can kiss your little monkey tail good-bye. Because this will fix you!"

Elvis raised the mirror and turned its clear face toward me.

I looked into the mirror. And there was my own monkey face. It was one small face in the mirror. And behind my clenched jaw and bared teeth, I could see my own fear, deep behind my eyes.

I began to feel woozy. I realized it was the mirror at work.

"Do you still think you're a tiger?" laughed Elvis, pushing the mirror closer to my face.

I was feeling very tired. Then I heard a new voice.

"He's not, but I am," said an animal from behind the crowd of baboons that surrounded me.

In one movement, all the baboon heads, including Elvis', turned to find this voice.

And they saw a great white tiger.

"So let's get acquainted" said Gabur. Then the great tiger leapt at the baboons sending them squawking and scrambling in all directions.

Like a house cat leaping on mice, Gabur darted forward, hooking a baboon with his claws then killing it with a single shake of his mouth. He then leapt forward and did the same to his next victim, scurrying from hopping baboon to baboon, as the pack screamed and fled in panic. Elvis had put the mirror to his chest and was running with all his might toward the baboon's mountain of slag for safety.

Six astral baboons lay dead and mangled on the ground as Gabur charged away after the fleeing pack.

Although they were dead, I knew they would be back the next day.

After a minute, Gabur came trotting back to me.

He sat, smiled at me, then began licking a paw as casually as if nothing had happened.

"You saved me?" I said.

"Sure," laughed Gabur. I could actually hear a low rumbling in his throat. He was purring, he was pleased with himself.

"Why? I thought you didn't travel in your astral body anymore."

"Well, I don't," said Gabur, "but I thought perhaps I would check in on you. And besides, slaughtering baboons is always fun."

I grimaced. It had not been much fun for me.

"The mirror is still unbroken," I said.

"Yes," said Gabur. A brilliant white stream of sunlight broke like a searchlight beam falling into the zoo grounds, lighting the wall of the primate house.

Gabur looked hastily around. "I must go. Good luck, little monk; they'll be back. Remember what I said: with a tiger's heart, look through the mirror. See what you want. I wish you luck in breaking it."

And then the astral being of the great white tiger stepped into the sunlight and disappeared.

"Remember your promise," came from an ethereal voice.

I got up and limped for the monkey house.

Chapter 124

That morning, when I woke, I found my shoulder whole. Dream wounds and my drubbing by the baboons had not stayed with me. All morning and into the afternoon, I paced nervously in my glass enclosure, occasionally looking into the vacant cage across the way. Vacant because I knew where Jacko really was.

I had a strong sense of time running out. The baboons now were quite formidable, and it had taken Gabur the White Tiger to drive them from their prey.

Yet the hallways of the primate house were strangely quite. Even the day's visitors were taking quick glances over their shoulders as they walked. A sickness was in the zoo, and though the human visitors had no inkling of what it really was, they could feel the tenseness of the animals sitting stiff and watchful in their cages, and they sensed something was out of the ordinary. Something eerie and troubling.

The visitors walked tentatively, casting looks of suspicion at the glass walls about them.

I expect the only animals that were playing merrily that day were the baboons on their heap.

It was not until afternoon that I noticed the change in Tanya's cage. There on the floor was a scattering of sticks and twigs. Tanya was sitting huddled in her corner her head down as if staring at something between her feet. Then I noticed she wasn't moving. A thought occurred to me. I looked into the leafy tree trunk near the skylight at the top of her cage. The sparrow's nest was gone. I realized it was covering the cement floor. I wondered why Tanya would do that, then a sudden chill went down my spine.

As I looked into her corner, I could see Tanya was indeed asleep. Unmoving.

I watched with rising unhappiness as Tanya sat head down as if staring at something.

And then I looked closely. And there was something between her feet.

It was the body of a sparrow, lying on its back, still as a stick.

Those damned baboons.

I leaned my forehead against the glass of my cage. It was like someone had filled my stomach with cold water. It was a dull cold weight.

Evening and the time of dreams finally came. I slept and as an astral animal left my body. I was not sure if this would be for the last time.

As I left my cage, I found the normal riotous sounds of the zoo were again stilled. When I slipped out of the primate house and tread uneasily toward the concession stand, where normally I would have seen a menagerie of animals at play, now the zoo grounds were abandoned. The zoo's many astral beings knew that the baboons were the source of the current terrors and so few animals were venturing forth. They could be seen sticking close within their cages, next to their sleeping bodies, as watchful and silent as tracked animals.

Yet, wherever I looked, I saw baboons walking at ease between buildings, sitting on rooftops, playing in the playground. Somehow this single species seemed to have come to dominate all the zoo.

How could such power come from a piece of glass?

The astral zoo looked a forlorn place.

I hastened my trot to check on Kory's and Jacko's bodies. I wanted to make sure they were still all right.

But a strong feeling gripped me as I stealthily crossed the zoo.

I finally could stand it no longer.

I climbed to the top of a tall pine, one that overlooked all the zoo, above the tiger pit. And from this high perch, I made what I thought might be my last call. I didn't care what baboon heard me.

"Oh, Astral zoo,
I see you
you animals locked in your cages
forced to sleep by day,
forced to travel in darkness by night
I see you,
I see you

and know,
your suffering is great."

Chapter 125

I kept close to the hedges and flowerbeds as I stole my way across the zoo. I ducked back under the bushes whenever I saw a baboon walking sentry around one of the zoo buildings. I came around a corner to find the zebra-striped golf cart parked nosed into one of the refreshment kiosks. There, sitting in the driver seat was Godzilla. The old gorilla was asleep with his head and arms draped over the wheel.

Grimly I knew the baboons had gotten him.

There was nothing I could do for him, so I hurried on. Finally I came to the igloo of lilac bushes where Kory's body lay. I crept under the low branches hoping the baboons had not discovered her sleeping body. I was afraid they might hurt her further in some way.

I approached Kory and sat down. As I squatted next to her, I could see her breathing shallowly in her sleep. She didn't move as I sat beside her. I took my tail and wiped some of lilac flowers from her coat.

Then I wept a little bit, hiding my eyes in this same tail.

Finally, I knew my longing for her to wake would never have any effect and I got up to leave.

"See you in my next dream," I said.

I hoped that dream would be a happier one.

I came out from under the bushes and began loping toward the trash pit. I felt my heart dictate that I must run to this pit or die. I scampered over benches, walls, and the last fence, until I reached the awful pit.

At its edge, I looked down on Jacko.

He lay prostrate on his back, arms out, as if sunbathing.

I hung on edge of the pit, then dropped down to be with him. I found myself squatting, inspecting this nearly dead animal.

"Jacko, I have seen Gabur. And as you said, I have gone beneath the zoo and met the great snake, Kunda," I said to the sleeping face. "But I don't know, what I have learned, will it make any difference?"

I sat for a moment in silence. I could see, sitting beside the sleeping Jacko, it would never make any difference here. In frustration, I grabbed his hairy shoulder and shook it.

"Help me! Wake up!" I shouted.

But the old ape only lay there. I couldn't stir him. I knew it was useless. Then I looked and saw Jacko's head was turned as if to look at one of his hands. The paw was balled in a fist.

I hopped over to the closed paw. There was something in it.

Carefully I pried open the boney fingers. There, in his leathery palm was a large reddish stone. It was smooth and the size and shape of a chicken's egg.

It was a beautiful thrower. Precisely the kind my old grandfather Chok would have instructed me to select.

I picked up the stone. Then I ran and leapt to haul myself out of the pit.

Chapter 126

I crossed between the insect house and the elephant barracks. There in the sidewalk was a slow moving hump, like a washtub walking the zoo grounds. It was Adam, a hundred-year-old land tortoise that walked the zoo. He was nearly blind, and had stopped speaking to us animals years ago. He would simply lay down and withdraw into his hardened shell at any approach.

Most of us zoo animals had no use for him. With him nearly blind, impervious to attack, I realized there was little the baboons could do to him. So he was out trundling around. Yet, I knew he could never break the mirror and it seemed a hardened useless old life.

As I bustled past him, heading for the baboon slag, Adam did not even turn his head my way.

As I rounded the corner of the primate house, I saw the Baboon heap on the far side of the plaza. Buck, stationed atop the concession stand, hooted three times. Several other baboon heads appeared on roof tops to stare at me. I continued hopping forward toward the slag heap. It's broken concrete and blackened rocks formed a slumped tower before me. And there a single baboon sat atop the slag.

As I neared the edge of the heap, the wall that kept the visitors out of the baboon pit, I began to walk. I was breathing guardedly in and out. I didn't want the baboons to see me panting in fear.

With a hoot the single baboon at the top of the heap disappeared down behind the rocks.

"Elvis," I shouted, "Elvis, King of the Slag monkeys!" I shouted.

A dozen baboons had jogged up to sit in a row like crows on the low wall surrounding the heap. Each was nudging the other and making fun of me, grunting, swaggering, and showing their teeth.

"Elvis, come out, and bring your mirror," I shouted.

Now, twenty large baboons flooded over the top and down the slag heap. Trotting at the head was Elvis. He had a big grin on his face as he loped with the mirror clutched to his chest.

"Be there in a minute, nut eater," shouted Elvis with glee. "I guess it is time for your second dose."

At the sight of the pack coming my way, I felt the urge to fall back quickly.

But I remembered Gabur's urgings to look on with a tiger's heart. I stiffened my resolve, letting my anger rise in me.

"Well, just one puny rockthrower?" said Elvis as he stopped some ten feet in front of me. "I remember back in the jungle I used to bite the asses of dozens in a single battle before I thought it was a good day."

I squeezed the red rock in my fist. I didn't want to move my hand for fear of calling attention to the stone.

"Them was fun days," shouted Elvis to his crowd. "But now, instead of bites, we have a better weapon. One that is perfect. One that is indestructible. One that freezes their souls! Ha!" laughed Elvis.

"So say, birdshit," called Randall from back on the heap, "Why don't you just get out of the zoo!"

At this the baboon pack laughed. They knew no zoo animal could ever leave, and soon the zoo would be theirs.

"Well," shrugged Elvis, "If you can't slay the pack, let the pack slay the one. Let's get this over with, rocks-for-brains."

"And here it is!"

Elvis turned the mirror toward me.

"There! Look in you puny little pebble-flicker. Here is the true picture of you. A mewling little shit bag in monkey fur!" At that insult, all the surrounding baboons began cawing encouragement to Elvis.

And I couldn't help it. I looked in the mirror. And sure enough, there I was. And, to me, it was a sorry sight. A single rockthrower, worried, tracked, hunched before the mirror.

I could feel dizziness setting in.

"And there he goes!" shouted Elvis, seeing my eyes trained into his glass.

"Look through," I heard in my head. "With a tiger's heart, look through." I heard it in the voice of a tiger in my ear.

I raised my anger level in my chest. I stood up on my hind legs.

I called once: "Boons and goons, now there's a true rhyme!"

Elvis laughed, "Oh yes, now that really hurt my old baboon heart, calling me a goon. Bless your little goon mother!"

Now the whole baboon pack was riotous with calls and cawing aimed at me.

The mirror shone toward me. It kept pulling my gaze back into it. I could now see a little monkey stood up on its hindlegs, tail flagging in the air behind. I began to feel dizzy again.

"Look through and see what you want," I heard again.

And then, my insides were alight. I looked at the mirror, and in my mind I saw what I wanted. I could feel my chest heating up, I could feel my eyes beginning to glow with the same fiery light that I had seen in Gabur's eyes. I looked and in my fear and anger, my eyes growing red with energy, I gazed not at myself in the mirror, but beyond to the Temple Arkteepa. I saw it glistening in my heart, golden in the new dawn, just as I had loved it.

"Give it up, rock-sucker," sneered Elvis, "It doesn't hurt and it doesn't take long. Suck in the power of the mirror."

But as I stood up, with the vision of Arkteepa in my mind, I could hear the other baboons quieting. They had never seen an animal last this long before.

"Give it up!" screamed Elvis. He held the mirror higher over my head so that I could see only its face.

"I dibs pulling off his tail!" shouted Buck viciously from the fence.

Arkteepa! Akteepa, I said in my head, trying to keep its vision focused before me. If I let it go now, I knew I would die, reflecting and dying by the violence before me.

And then I heard another voice. The voice of a snake.

"Sing the song. Sing my song."

And with my heart full of anger, my vision filled with the temple, I opened my mouth and began to sing the song of the Great Lily.

The long old song of my tribe.

With the heart of a tiger, with glowing eyes, I sang the song that my mother had taught me, the song Chok had wanted me to sing when I threw my rocks.

The song with Kunda at its heart.

The baboons were looking from one to another. This had never happened before. An animal bursting into a song. They sat to listen, many sneering.

I sang the song of the Great Lily, not knowing what I would do or where it would lead. I sang for Kory, for Jacko, for the beautiful and lonely Gabur, for the powerful and feared Kunda below the zoo. I sang for my long lost mother, for the loyal guard of my far away father the Watcher, and I sang for the remembered monkey warmth of Chok.

With the song, I felt a unity within that I had never known. The unity of Keth's strong light and Binah's dark light shining over us all, always.

And as I sang the last of the song, I felt the mirror release me.

Chapter 127

And then I was just a monkey. I sat down, calmly. The spell of the mirror had broken. I could still feel Gabur's spirit burning in my heart. And I knew that as I acted so the baboons in front of me would act. I sat calmly. And a silence entered the baboon pack. They slowly stopped hooting and jeering, seeing their target had changed demeanor, was not ranting back at them. I was just a single monkey, and myself. I realized that this pack surrounding me meant nothing to me. I could simply run off and get away. I could out run them, hide, do anything I wanted. And even if they caught me later, tore me to pieces, it meant nothing. As long as I didn't look in the mirror, didn't see what they wanted me to see, then I would spring back to life again. As long as I was myself, seeing what I wanted to see, I would be fine.

And then I knew my duty. I couldn't run away, leaving my companions and loved ones caught by the mirror, asleep, caught in unconsciousness that led slowly but certainly to death. I had to break the mirror.

And as I felt Gabur's tiger heart, his spirit, still hardened within me, as I sternly looked behind the mirror at the bewildered baboons watching me, wondering why the mirror had not worked, as I looked beyond to my desire, the beauty of Arkteepa, I still heard the song of my Mother, the song my grandfather Chok told me to sing in battle, the song of the Great Lily, and knew I was just another monkey.

Clasping Jacko's reddish stone in my hand, I realized that the mirror had worked perfectly.

I was just another monkey.

And I was a rockthrower.

And so I threw.

Chapter 128

Elvis squawked and jumped back as the mirror shattered in his paws. My throw had been true. He tottered, left holding a single large splinter, the shape of a fang, as the rest of mirror clinked and tinkled in pieces on the sidewalk. The baboon crowd watched wide-eyed.

The mirror was broken.

Elvis, outraged, was left gripping the largest shard.

"You miserable flea bag! You mangy hairless tail wagger! What have you done!"

He was screaming at me in anger. But bewildered, he was now backing up toward the baboon slag, trying to save this one piece of mirror that was left. I was sure he hoped that this one fragment was large enough to still be used.

Elvis scampered for safety to the middle of the slag mountain. He began calling to his hoards to follow him in retreat.

"I will come back and kill you personally!" screamed Elvis back down at me. The baboon pack was now regrouping slowly, stunned by the breaking of the mirror. They were moving to the base of the baboon mountain to look up at their angry leader above.

And then at the top of the mountain, above and behind Elvis still ranting and protesting down to me, I saw a movement. A great head rose like a black pole at top of the slag heap.

It was Kunda, the snake.

And in his mouth, he held something hanging limp.

Kunda's head rose, and as I watched, and the baboon crowd cowered, Elvis slowly turned to find in surprise a great snake behind him. Then I saw that Kunda held the body of a large baboon in his mouth.

He shook it like a flag and began to swallow it.

Elvis screamed as he recognized the baboon body.

Elvis screeched as he saw his own body disappearing into the snake's mouth.

I realized that this Kunda was not an astral projection. He was the real snake, come into the zoo in the night. Although we saw him in astral day, Kunda was there alive and alone in the blackness. He was a real being in the zoo that we astral beings were powerless to effect. He had stolen into the zoo and into the baboon grounds and grabbed Elvis' sleeping body.

And the body was now disappearing shoulder, by hip, by foot, by tail down the snake's gulping maw.

Elvis was bleating in fear and panic.

Then Elvis disappeared.

The last shard of the mirror fell and broke.

Chapter 129

I hustled to the flowering lilac where I had left Kory. I rushed under the low brush, the ground scattered with purple blossoms, to enter the hollow.

There I found Kory sitting up blinking and looking around.

I sat before her, afraid to speak, tears brimming my eyes.

"Hello," said Kory. "I know you." Then she managed a smile.

I gulped, but could say nothing. Kory was awake and alive.

"I seemed to have fallen asleep. Was I asleep long?" asked Kory.

I nodded.

Kory looked around her mystified to find herself in new surroundings.

She hesitated, I could see her mind feeling out for what had happened to her.

"But I'm awake now," she said.

I nodded.

"Why do you look so trashed?" said Kory, inspecting my face.

I shook my head and mustered a smile.

"Did you miss me, fur ball?" she laughed still mystified.

"Oh, yes," I said.

Chapter 130

I led Kory out beneath the lilacs and to the back of the zoo, there to find Jacko sitting up groggily in the pit.

As Kory and I hopped down and approached him, the old orang looked up at us.

He smiled.

"You must have done it," he said to me.

"Yes," I said.

"The mirror is broken?" asked Kory.

"Yes," I said.

"How did you do it?" cried Jacko with glee.

"You broke the mirror?" asked Kory again, incredulous. "How?"

"I am just a rockthrower, so I threw," I shrugged.

"And how did you get that mark on your chest?"

I looked down to see Kunda's mark of the Great Lily.

"It happened in the dark," I said. "I'll tell you that story later."

Kory and I led the limping Jacko back through the morning light to the primate house. Jacko pulled open the heavy metal door and we entered. We went to Jacko's cage, three animals in our full flesh and blood, to wait for the zookeepers to arrive. We knew they would be surprised to find three animals waiting to be let back into their cages.

Then the primate house was filled with howling. The echoes of each strong howl rang off the primate house walls.

I looked at Jacko and Kory and we all went to look in the cage next door at the sound's source.

It was Tanya. She had waken, and was now howling, swinging, and flying about her cage. She was doing flips, swinging by her tail, and generally ricocheting about her enclosure.

And there on Tanya's cage floor flitted a sparrow, boldly looking about.

Tanya was awake and her sparrow back.

Tanya was caroming off her cage walls with all her might and all her joy.

"I guess she knows what it means to be an animal," laughed Jacko.

Chapter 131

Now I live in the zoo. I live a full life as any, Kory and I together at night, playing among the other dream animals. To the astonishment of the zookeepers, Kory has even had a little monkey girl, one who can both leap like crazy and throw rocks.

The zookeepers are spooked with rumors of an immaculate conception! Kory and I laugh quite a bit at that.

Jacko, he lives comfortably in his bell tower.

And each morning, the zookeepers find the zebra-striped golf cart parked in a new place as they always did.

We don't have much trouble with the baboons. Without the mirror, they are just one more brand of animal in the zoo.

My dreams during the day, they turn more and more toward my homeland, Arkteepa. A place to which I will never return.

To quell my heart, I sometimes climb to the highest branches. And there I call the rockthrower call.

I sing of the animals in the zoo.

I sing of the joy and peace I see.

I sing of my love and loved ones.

I call to the animal folk like me.

I sing of the baboons, animals who lost their way, lost the true source of their light, thought it came reflected from a mirror.

And for me, one thing is clear.

The song is the secret.

The real weapon is the song. The song that unites the seer and the seen, that unites the seer and the unseen.

So I live beneath both the shining lights of Keth and Binah.

I accept Kunda's dark power.

And someday, I know I must go back and visit the lonely Gabur.

None of us are born to be in cages, but each of us gets there. It seems unlikely that the zoo will ever become Arkteepa. The zookeepers' vision would have to change so radically. But as the years pass, it does get better. I see improvements in the zoo. As the zookeepers get better educated about us animals, as their consciousness rises.

As they become closer to astral beings.

I, Tip, mighty rockthrower, live in the astral zoo.

www.ingramcontent.com/pod-product-compliance
Lightning Source LLC
LaVergne TN
LVHW050644100826
845148LV00011B/1977
* 9 7 8 0 6 1 5 5 8 4 7 2 0 *